SHILLING & FLORIN

BOOK THREE:
A DALLIANCE WITH GRIEF

KATE HALEY

ISBN: 978-1-991364-02-9 (paperback)
978-1-991364-03-6 (kindle)
978-1-991364-18-0 (hardcover)

Cover design by Kate Haley

WARNING:
This book is darker than the previous books,
but trust me — I know what I'm doing.
Let me cook.

CONTENTS

Visit **www.katehaleyauthor.com** for
deals and current news from the author.

1

Water dripped in slow but constant trickles down the walls. The sound of it echoed in the tunnels, but was drowned out by the rushing of pipes. Those sounds drowned out other, less savoury, noises. A bang. A rattle. Whimpering. Humming.

The water began clean, trickling over the stones. A small mercy. It eased the smell. In the dark, it was impossible to know what other liquids coated the walls, thick with moss and grime. It was impossible to see the blood in the dark, as it mixed with the water, and washed away all evidence of its existence.

The day was bleak with drizzle. Rain came on and off in thin, weak, half-hearted patches. It was an excellent day for a funeral — if such a thing existed. Charlie hated funerals. He avoided them wherever he could, which hadn't been quite so easy of late. The first funeral he ever remembered attending was his father's. He'd been too young to remember his mother's funeral. That was probably a blessing.

Recently, all the funerals he had attended were for victims of the Jack of Hearts. They had been harrowing, nasty affairs, but he had gone to most, not just because the women were usually acquaintances, but because he had been hunting their killer and any clue could have helped.

Now, he was attending the Jack's own funeral.

The notion was insane, but hopefully it would be the final nail in the coffin, literally. Lord Pound had given him every access, and Charlie had come up empty handed. There was no note. Nothing new. Perhaps the clue had been in one of the letters Harry had written to Florin, but she'd burnt them all without reading them, so he would never know. Not that he begrudged her that. Not in the slightest. By all accounts and evidence, Harry had hanged himself in his cell just days before he was due to go to trial.

It did make sense, Charlie was prepared to admit, even if he didn't want to say that to Pound and Florin. He didn't have to. They knew.

Henry had asked him to accompany them today. Asked seemed the appropriate word, although Charlie had found Pound's request that he accompany Florin halfway between a beg and an order. Henry was worried about his daughter. Charlie was worried about her too. That didn't mean he thought this was right.

His first stop was just across the road. The bakery was quiet this morning. Terry gave him a once over with his eyes and sent him upstairs without a word. The door to Mike's room was open and the space looked trashed. Charlie raced the last few stairs and charged in.

"What happened?!" he demanded. "Has anything been stolen?!"

Michael Pence was probably the single largest retailer of information in the city. Most people didn't know that and his business ran underground, but if anyone wanted to know something, he would have been the person to go to. He was a constant source of aid to Charlie, and his notes regarding Harry's death had been helpfully accurate, as far as Charlie had been able to deduce.

Mike looked up from behind the desk, where he had been gathering and stacking piles of notes, his face flushed at Charlie's concern. There were two other people in the room. Mike's boyfriend Julian was adjusting his tie in front of a small mirror and Mike's brother John was leaning against one of the upright filing cabinets. John smirked as soon as Charlie appeared.

"Yes, we thought they were being attacked too," he commented drolly. "Apparently this qualifies as enthusiasm rather than assault."

"You're not supposed to trash his stuff, Swift," Charlie told Julian, glancing his way.

"I didn't trash anything," Julian grinned at his reflection, combing back his thick dark curls. "It was a mutual effort."

"The word you used earlier was 'magnificent'," John teased.

"It was that too," Julian smirked, shooting him a wink.

Charlie ignored them to refocus his attention.

Michael was understandably more flustered than usual. He was out of his baking uniform and his clothes were neat and dark. It was a strange juxtaposition, that he was presented tidier while losing his usual composure.

"I've never seen you in black, Skipp," Charlie told him.

"It's Julian's," Mike replied, barely looking up as he sorted at speed. "I'm just borrowing it. Never seen you in so much black either."

"It felt inappropriate to wear anything else," Charlie sighed, reaching into his coat pocket and pulling out a hipflask. "Buggered if I know who I'm supposed to be mourning though." He took a drink.

John quirked an eyebrow at him. "Bit early, isn't it?"

"Not today," Charlie shook his head. He drained the flask. "I promised I'd go. I promised Pound I'd show up early. But I shouldn't be there. It's not my place."

"Actually, it is, Sleuth," Julian disagreed, finishing with the mirror and turning to him. "I get why you don't want to, but it is your place. You helped Amy put him behind bars. Now you gotta help her put him in the ground."

"I know," Charlie sighed, shaking the empty flask sadly. "I just really, really, really don't want to."

"What are you drinking?" Julian checked.

"Whatever I nicked off Susan," Charlie shrugged. "It's not working."

"It won't, Sleuth," Julian chuckled at him. "Your sister's a lightweight and she drinks like it. Here," he grabbed a bottle from a trunk under the bed on his side of the room, "this will sort you out." Julian took the flask and filled it liberally from his whisky collection.

"Julian, darling, he's supposed to be looking after Florin. Don't get him drunk," Michael protested from the desk.

"I don't think I'll survive this completely sober," Charlie commented. "Skipp, do you need a hand?"

"I've got this," he replied automatically.

Charlie understood, but he also didn't want to leave his friend struggling while the other two watched. He approached and, without asking, began sorting the collection of upended files into the correct piles on Mike's desk.

"Thanks Sleuth." Mike shot him a half-smile, running a stack of files to one of the cabinets John was leaning by.

"How come he's allowed to help?" Julian protested. "You told me I couldn't."

"It's Sleuth, darling, he knows what he's doing," Mike countered instantly. Julian pulled a sad face at him as he went by. Michael paused, stopping to kiss Julian's cheek as he passed him. "I love you. Don't touch anything."

Julian rolled his eyes and took a swig from his bottle. John watched them all curiously.

"Why are you all going to this funeral if no one wants to be there?" he asked.

"That's an excellent question," Michael sighed, making sure everything on the desk was clearly labelled. "Now — info, inquiries, misc.; everything is divided by area and ascending class order. I've told all the runners I'm out this morning, but they can still drop off if they absolutely have to. These are outs and I have written names, passcodes, and prices on them. Only if someone is able to give the name, passcode and pay the full amount do you hand it over."

"Yes, Mikey, I get it," John huffed. "It's not hard."

"It is hard. Don't mess this up," Mike stressed.

"If you really don't trust me with it, we could swap?" John teased. "I'd be happy to keep Julian in line for the day instead."

"You couldn't handle me for five minutes," Julian taunted, sneaking up on Charlie and sliding his hands inside Charlie's coat to slip the hipflask away.

"But who wouldn't want the opportunity to try?" John smirked, watching him accost his small friend.

"Get your own," Michael scolded his brother. "Charlie, was there something you needed, or are you avoiding leaving for the Pound residence?"

"That is an excellent question," Charlie told him, having a cheeky peruse of the paperwork he was handling.

"Come on, Sleuth," Julian grinned, scooping him under the arms and lifting him off the ground. "You can't keep your lady waiting."

"She's not my lady," Charlie replied instantly.

Everyone else in the room rolled their eyes disparagingly. Charlie ignored that. They didn't know what they were talking about.

"What are you three going to do if she's dressed for a coronation?" John asked. "Celebratory flags waving?"

"She won't be," Charlie replied. "I was there when Henry told her what happened. Trust me, it might not have been the relationship the world thought it was before he was arrested, but Harry's death broke her. She's not celebrating anything."

"So you're going to support the good doctor and, what, these idiots are going to support you?" John asked, still trying to get to the bottom of why people were even attending.

"Something like that," Julian agreed.

"Julian's attending with Bronny and the ladies," Charlie countered. "Mike's going with him."

"We can support you too, Sleuth," Julian insisted. "Don't pretend like today isn't going to hurt."

"Wait—" John gave them all a suspicious look. "Bronny and the ladies…? This isn't a funeral, it's a protest!"

"It can be both," Charlie sighed. He continued to hang limply from Julian's arms, still scanning the file in his hands. It wasn't interesting. The hug was nice though. "Henry's made sure there will be a sizable police presence. Hopefully nothing gets out of hand."

"Good luck," John grimaced, no longer offering to attend in anyone's place.

"Thank you," Charlie sighed. "I'm sure we'll need it."

"Sleuth, you're starting to get very heavy," Julian insisted, shaking him slightly in an effort to make him stand on his own two feet.

"But I'm weak and you smell good," Charlie sighed.

Julian laughed and kissed his cheek. "Stand up, Charles."

Charlie did as he was told, planting his feet so that

Julian could let him go, although he was notably reluctant. Julian gave him a consoling pat as he dropped him.

"Doesn't concern you when it's him?" John said pointedly to his brother, eyeing Julian and Charlie.

"No," Mike replied. "Those two are what we would be if you weren't so annoying."

"And if you weren't such an arrogant twat," John replied in kind.

Charlie and Julian shared a look. Charlie knew that look. It was a knowing look. That was the look that conveyed how annoying he was, and that Julian was an arrogant twat. The Pence siblings had yet to catch on. Julian winked at him.

"Shouldn't you be off, Sleuth?" he commented. "Especially if you're supposed to be meeting our good doctor beforehand."

Charlie glowered. He finished setting down the notes and took a sip from his refilled flask. The new drink immediately made him cough. It was impossible to hide, try though he might, even though he knew Julian would laugh at him. Apparently, Julian was feeling generous today. He settled for a gentle snicker and a comforting pat on the back.

"He's right, Charlie," Mike insisted. "Florin needs you today."

Charlie thought about arguing. It was one of his greatest talents, after all. But he thought of Florin, standing with him on the ferry back to England just a few days ago, holding onto his arm. She did need a friend today, and it was selfish of him to deny her that just because the ordeal made him uncomfortable. Everyone had to do things they didn't like sometimes. He might as well do it to help someone he loved.

He sighed and straightened his coat, pocketing the now dangerous hipflask.

"Still weird seeing you in black, Sleuth," Mike smiled.

"Weirder still for you, Skipp," Charlie replied. "Susan and Becky will be taking the carriage to Bronny's later. You should get a ride with them. They won't mind."

"Uh—" Mike started to hesitate.

"Thanks Sleuth," Julian grinned at him. "Very kind of you. Tell me you're not going to walk to Lord Pound's house in the rain."

"It's just drizzle," Charlie shrugged. "The walk isn't far, and there's plenty of cover."

"So you're going to show up on her doorstep, dripping wet, to support her through her ex's funeral?" Julian shook his head helplessly, still grinning. "This is why Lionel writes stories about you two."

"Lionel's an idiot," Charlie retorted. "Do not give that man any credence. I walk everywhere. This isn't special."

"You're cutting it a touch fine, maybe take the Underground?" John suggested.

Charlie looked like he'd just suggested polishing his shoes with dung. He could see Michael and Julian trying to subtly shake their heads at him.

"I'm walking," he insisted stubbornly. There might

have been more to the conversation, but he didn't want to know what it was. He left them to it and headed downstairs before anyone could suggest any more terrible ideas. Terry gave him one more nod and let him swipe a pastry on his way out. It made the morning considerably more tolerable.

2

It felt like all the colour had been washed from the world. The dismal weather stained everything grey and sapped the beauty from the landscape. Everyone was wearing black. It had only been a few days, but everyone Amy saw just wore black. She was sick of it.

She was sick of grieving.

It felt like all she'd been doing for months now. There had been that brief, shining moment in France… but that felt a lifetime ago now. It felt like a whole other world, somewhere she'd visited in a dream and no longer knew how to get back to. She had written to Argent already and told him what had happened. He would, of course, already know. He did get English papers. But she had promised to write, she wanted to write, and that distant letter she'd posted felt like the only lifeline to a world beyond this broken one.

She wasn't sad that Harry was dead. It was a good thing. It saved them the agony of the trial. It was justice. She kept telling herself that. It made sense. This was good.

So why was she such a mess? Why was she so hurt? Why was she so angry she could scream? Why did it feel like that all the time? And why was there this unrelenting pressure building in her chest that just kept growing and growing and growing, until it felt like she was going to erupt with all the power and agony of Vesuvius and lay waste to the entire city?!

She took a deep, trembling breath and blinked slowly. The view of the back garden through the window should have been calming. Unfortunately, nothing was. There was just this constant searing agony, barely contained and thinly veiled. She wanted to tear down the world and rebuild it, with absolutely no trace or memory of Henry Pound Junior.

AKA The Jack of Hearts.

AKA her Harry.

She pinched her lips together and stifled a retch. The last thing she needed was to vomit all over her windowsill. As soon as her stomach settled, she took another deep breath. She could do this. She just had to get through today and then, maybe, the world might leave her alone for a bit. Maybe then she could escape somewhere else. Maybe then she could find the time, find the space, to tell her father about Argent. Maybe even take him to visit.

There had to be something else. But there was nothing. She couldn't make herself feel anything. There was a letter beside her. *Dear Florence Pound, we are delighted to accept your manuscript on behalf of Dawson & Kropp… etc.* She'd read it ten times since she received it yesterday afternoon. She felt nothing. It should have been elating… but the hard nausea in her gut drowned everything else.

There was a knock at the door. She sighed and

turned to face it. She hadn't closed her room off. If she kept it open, it stayed public. It helped her hold in the rage. Penny, one of the maids, stood hesitantly in the doorway, looking in with nervous eyes, as though she didn't want to interrupt. There was nothing to interrupt. Amy hadn't been doing anything.

"Yes?" Amy inquired with cool detachment.

"Pardon the intrusion, Doctor," Penny murmured. "You have a visitor."

"Tell them to leave," Amy ordered. She had told her friends not to come early today. Jane and Laura, bless them, were the most understanding and sympathetic people in the world, and she just couldn't cope with that now. She didn't want to be coddled. She didn't want to be reasoned with by people trying to help her.

"Forgive me, Doctor," Penny begged. "Apparently Lord Pound requested him here, but his Lordship is presently busy. He suggested I send him to you."

"Him?" Amy echoed numbly, a faint stirring beneath her ribs, in the depths of her soul. She didn't know why she'd asked such a stupid parroting question. She knew who 'him' meant.

"Mister Shilling is downstairs," Penny replied. "I set him to wait in the library—"

"I'll be down in a moment," Amy blurted, hating the sudden urgency in her voice. The sharp blush that followed was an abrupt warmth that she hadn't realised her cold body needed. "Actually, Penny, it's Charlie. Maybe bring him some tea and a scone, if you have it."

"Of course, Doctor," Penny smiled, giving a small curtsy and hurrying off.

Goddamn, even the help threw small smiles about behind their backs. They all knew. The problem was she hadn't been subtle about it. She hadn't known to be subtle. She'd gone straight from barely knowing the man to falling for him in the space of a breath, and somewhere in there she had taken to treating him as familiarly as her best friends of many years. It didn't take a genius. It didn't take Shilling. Although, mercifully, he didn't seem to have noticed. He probably just thought she was strange and left it at that.

She took a moment to compose herself. It wouldn't do to go flying down the stairs to see him the instant he arrived. Some last vestige of dignity should be maintained. Besides, he hadn't come to see her. He was here because her father had invited him. It wasn't like Charlie to drop by unannounced to see her unless he was working. Although, he had informed her the day before they left for France that he had attempted to visit, before being overcome with anxiety.

It worried her slightly. For all that he was admirably useful, Charlie seemed to be under the impression he was a nuisance to everyone. It was easy to believe he was always treated as such. While clearly unafraid to be said nuisance, it was just as clear he didn't want to be.

The second she felt she could face him without dissolving into tears, Amy moved stoically from her room to the library. Her chest was tight and her jaw clenched, but it was the best she was going to get today. Except seeing him weakened all of it. Seeing him standing there, through the doorway, dressed all in black, was a fresh kind of heartbreak. He didn't suit black. It made him look pale, almost sickly. His hair was darker than normal. Damp. He must have walked here in the rain. He wasn't soaked, but he was loitering near the books, eyeing the shelves, like he dare not touch them in case the droplets sparkling amongst the woollen fibres of his jacket were to spring off and attack the pages.

He paused suddenly, cocking his head to the side and turning to the doorway. He must have heard her approach, or somehow realised she was near. There was a solemn slant to his eyes and the crooked line of his mouth exacerbated the gravity of the atmosphere like a frown. He started towards her, hesitant but concerned. The hesitation won when he was halfway across the room, pausing as though only just noticing he was still wet.

"Florin, you poor thing, how are you?" he murmured, hands linking together uncertainly and fingers beginning to twist his signet ring.

She watched him fidget for a moment. That was the ring that had started so much of this. She had watched him fidget with it all day when they had been hunting the Jack. So she had recognised the seal bruised into Harry's cheek when he had shown up wounded in her bedroom. Charlie was always fidgeting with something. His brain was busy, so his hands needed to be busy, and if they weren't, if he didn't know what to do with himself or how to behave, he got anxious.

Amy crossed the last few steps between them. His hands were forced apart as she moved into his space, slipping her arms around his waist and burying her face in the collar of his black coat. She squeezed him, letting the water from his coat soak into her sleeves. He hugged her back. His arms were sure and tight around her shoulders, and his cheek rested gently against hers. A few loose strands of his messy, damp hair felt cold and wet against the top of her ear. She turned into it, as though to kiss his cheek, even though she knew she shouldn't.

She wanted to.

The feel of him in their shared embrace was the only thing holding her together. If he let go, if he spoke, if anything moved to break this, she would fly apart. She held on as tight as she could, breathing in the scent of him. He smelled like rain and soot and lavender. Lavender and rose and chamomile…?

"Charlie…" she whispered into his collar, "are you wearing my perfume?"

"No," he muttered.

"Is that whisky on your breath?" She started to pull away.

"No…" he muttered. There was a notable strain to the 'no', quickly followed by a pained "yes… but it's not working!"

She laughed at him as she let him go. A minute ago the idea of laughing had been impossible. But there was something about Charlie. He didn't mean it. He was trying his best. He was just a little bit hopeless in the most endearing way she could imagine. She didn't take her hands from his waist as she pulled her body back from his, and watched his little face scrunch up ruefully.

"I'm sorry, Florin," he muttered, still holding her

gently. "I don't want to be here. I shouldn't be here. Not for this. I don't belong at this funeral. It's not my place. I just wanted to take the edge off."

He let go then and Amy regretted drawing attention to it as he forced space between them, fumbling about. He pulled a silver hipflask from the depths of his coat, giving it a small shake which echoed a shallow slosh.

"I stole something from Susan after Becky took my cough syrup," he grumbled. "But I think it was more sugar water than alcohol, so I drank it all and it did nothing but spur hyperactivity, which seems to be manifesting as nervous energy, and then Julian gave me something he said would work better and I swear it is near undrinkable."

"Well, share it around then," Amy insisted, reaching for the flask. "You're not the only one with edges to take off."

She unscrewed the cap and sniffed the contents gently. A strong, rich scent filled her nose so powerfully she could feel it tingle her throat.

"This is very expensive Scottish whisky, Charlie," she declared.

"From Julian, I have no doubt," he pulled a face. "Expensive doesn't mean drinkable."

Amy took a sip. It coated her tongue and scalded her throat and put fire in her stomach. The heat spread through her chest, staving off the cold touch of death that had been creeping through her. The breath she let out was one she didn't even know she'd been holding. It flowed from her lungs, soft and hot and soothing.

"Oh... that's really good..." she murmured, casting

an appreciative glance at the flask in her hand.

Charlie gave her a dubious look. It made her smile. Looking at his messy hair, kind eyes, and crooked face, she couldn't believe there had ever been a time when she had found him even remotely unappealing. He was the sweetest thing. The doubt in his eyes was drowning in concern. It was hard not to just throw her arms around him and bury her face in his collar again.

"Charlie…" she began hesitantly, not sure what the rest of that sentence would be but knowing whatever it was she shouldn't say it.

His eyes narrowed and his head tilted slightly, but he was looking beyond her, out through the doorway. Amy stopped and turned. Penny stepped carefully into the room, wheeling a tray of tea and biscuits.

"Excuse me, Doctor," she murmured, quietly entering the room and setting up the refreshments on the coffee table.

Charlie's head was leaning slowly further and further to the side as he watched her, as though things would make sense if he could just get the right angle. Amy followed his gaze, trying to see what he saw. Penny kept her eyes demurely down and wouldn't look at them, but there was a small smile playing about her lips. An expression she was trying to hide. Her hands stayed busy, working in the background at tedious little tasks that didn't actually require her attention. She wasn't used to being noticed, but regular procedure didn't apply around Charlie.

"Sorry, Florin, you were about to say something?" he turned back to her just as sharply.

Amy felt her voice stick in her throat. She couldn't very well say anything now, not with an audience. Not that she'd known what she'd been about to say anyway. But it was almost certainly something she shouldn't say. Something she couldn't say.

"I just…" she whispered, hearing her own voice come out weak and wavering. She sounded hoarse. In a desperate attempt to stall, she sipped from the flask again. The sip turned into a swig almost instantly. Lady of Heaven, it was profoundly comforting. Not that she intended to drink all Charlie's whisky, but it was hard not to. She pulled the flask from her lips reluctantly and set the cap back on, taking a much needed breath. Her own eyes stared back at her from the brushed silver surface of the metal flask. "I haven't told Daddy about France…" she murmured to her reflection. The glint of light off the matching lid brought her back to reality, and she remembered Penny loitering nearby, eavesdropping, just as she had been by the door before Charlie caught on. "About what we found in France," she blurted additionally, suddenly worried what people might think.

"I'm not surprised," Charlie shrugged gently. He cast his eyes over the space, but nothing in his tone or posture shared Amy's concerns, even if he had been the first to notice they were being monitored. "Pound's been mourning his son. I can't imagine there's been a good time to raise the trouble I got you into in France."

"Charlie!" she exclaimed at his phrasing.

"What?" he looked to her in confusion.

Amy shook her head wearily, pressing her fingers to

her brow to keep them from reopening the flask in her other hand. She had a strong urge to drain it. With a sigh that willed all the patience she could muster, she looked up to meet his calm, grey eyes. They were deep and soulful, like an endless moment caught just before rain that would never fall. Then she realised she was turning into Julian and was forced to take another sip of whisky to stop herself from falling about laughing at her own foolishness.

"You never got me in trouble, Shilling," she announced softly, strengthened by the whisky.

"I took you to France," he muttered. "Even after I told you not to go with me."

"You never told me not to go with you!" Amy exclaimed. "You said I was helpful and welcome to accompany you!"

Charlie paused and considered this with a small, crooked frown.

"Hm. You are correct, Florin. I suppose I just thought it very loudly," he conceded.

Amy met Penny's eye. It was the final straw. Both women began to laugh, small but utterly helpless chuckles. Amy couldn't keep it together. Not today. Not standing here with Charlie, on the brink of Harry's funeral, being spied on by the maid, quite probably on her father's behalf. Not when Charlie was being so… Charlie.

Footsteps sounded in the hall, much stronger and louder than Penny's approach would ever have been. Amy immediately hid the flask she was holding behind her back. Henry Pound appeared in the doorway like the grim reaper. His suit was entirely black and his face was pale and pinched. Beneath his thick grey sideburns, Amy had noticed his face becoming gaunt of late. The shadows under his eyes were beginning to look like they would never fade.

"No need to stop on my account," he told the abruptly silent room. Even his voice was tired and thin.

Penny wouldn't look up again, and Amy didn't blame her for keeping busy and refusing to meet anyone's eye. She "finished" setting up the tea and excused herself. Amy wished she could do the same, not just to leave the room but to escape the situation. She wished she'd never left France.

"Thank you for coming, Mister Shilling," Henry shifted his attention.

"Of course, Pound," Charlie nodded, nervously smoothing his rumpled hair. "You told me to."

"I asked," Henry corrected.

"It had more of the hallmarks of an order than a request," Charlie replied in his characteristic blasé fashion, eyes already scouring the room again and fingers moving unconsciously to the buttons on his coat.

Amy held her breath, waiting for her father's sharp tone and harsh glare. One did not speak so to a Lord. However, his rebuke never came. Startlingly, the smallest of smiles touched the very corners of Henry's lips as he watched Shilling fidget uncomfortably.

"I thought you didn't conform to orders from the oppressive aristocracy?" Henry teased.

Charlie floundered. His eyes snapped back to Henry,

wide and startled, like a fawn caught in headlights. They found no answers there and Amy caught his glance as his gaze flicked between her and her father in a panic. She didn't know what she was missing, but she instantly knew there was something.

"You... said..." Charlie muttered anxiously. "You told me to..."

"Charlie," Henry cut him off firmly, his eyes still warmer than Amy had seen them since they returned to London. "Thank you."

"You're welcome..." Charlie replied, although a note of confusion still lingered about him.

"Was that so hard?" Henry pressed.

"Yes..." Charlie murmured anxiously.

Henry's lips parted as a genuine smile split his tired, grieving face. He looked to Amy and she felt the endless heartbreak in his eyes in the depths of her soul, but it was so good to see him smile again, even if only for a moment. It did make her wonder though. Something was at play. Probably something simple that she was too dazed to realise. Grief seemed to have slowed her wits, and she didn't know how to get them back. No matter how adamantly she told herself she shouldn't let any of this affect her.

"Daddy, why did you ask Charlie to join us today?" she asked.

"You told Laura and Jane not to meet you beforehand," he replied. "The decision was yours to make, but it concerned me. I wanted someone else here for you, if you needed them. Someone who cared."

And he'd picked Charlie?! She wanted to exclaim. Of

course he'd picked Charlie. Worse, Charlie had shown up. He wasn't obeying anyone or submitting to the whims of the aristocracy. He was here because he cared. He was only here because he cared. He wasn't always good at showing it. He struggled socially. He was erratic and inappropriate. But he cared about her. He cared enough to attend an event he desperately wanted to avoid, enough to wear black for a man he'd sent to prison, and enough to walk here in the rain for her.

Amy pulled the flask out from behind her back, unscrewed the cap, and began to drain it to keep herself from crying. She wasn't even sure why. But the tears were building and all she had to burn them away was really good whisky. It was not the kind of drink you were supposed to chug, and the pain that flared in the back of her throat was like a sobering slap in the face.

"Amelia!" her father snapped.

She held up a finger for the length of two gulps before she stopped. No one would dare manhandle a lady to interrupt her. Well, Charlie might, but she was fairly sure that she had permission to get away with anything in regard to him today. Now, that was a dangerous thought. She gasped as she took the flask from her lips and set the cap back over whatever dregs remained.

"Daddy, if people are going to talk to me today, if they're going to say things like that, then I need all the emotional defence I can get," she announced.

Henry looked to Charlie, who was already starting to try and blend into the upholstery.

"I take it that's yours?" he rebuked.

Charlie nodded reluctantly.

"I thought you preferred stronger substances, Shilling?"

"Rebecca's banned me from cough syrup," Charlie sighed. "So we make do. Alas, I am still as sober as a dying goat."

"It's possible the alcohol just hasn't had time to kick in," Amy told him.

Both men looked at her. She could see their eyes processing that while her statement could possibly contain a shred of truth for Charlie, it contained an entire barrel of truth for her.

"Can I interest you in some tea, Florin?" Charlie offered with an onset of sincere desperation.

She sighed at his show of concern and screwed the cap back on the flask properly, handing it back to him so she couldn't be tempted further.

"You needn't worry about me, Charlie," she muttered.

"That's impossible, Florin," he replied.

His sincerity gave her heart palpitations. The compassionate statement had swooped in before she could add that she was fine. Now she couldn't say it, because she wasn't. Goddamnit, this was why she had told her friends to stay away. The more they cared, the worse she felt. The more he cared, the more she worried she would simply keel over from the inability to process how she felt.

"Florin…" Charlie muttered, breaking her from her personal Hell, and stepping ever so slightly closer. "Please, Florin. We have to leave in a few minutes anyway, and there's no point letting the tea get cold."

She wanted to rebuke him that he always let his tea go cold, but there was no point. Today was a day of firsts anyway, and she imagined that by his standards it would be a day starved of adequate distractions. Today, tea was probably going to be the best distraction either of them got.

The day was still cold and wet and dismal. Charlie had not been privy to the arrangements for Harry's funeral, and he wasn't sure he wanted to be. He knew Henry had organised for a large police presence. He did not want to ask about the logistics. The ceremony was being held at the graveyard near the Pound family crypt where Harry would be entombed. Given the circumstances, no church was prepared to hold him, even though the family vicar would still provide the service.

Shilling expected a crowd. He hadn't expected quite such a crowd. The tension was suffocating. Half the crowd were there for Harry Pound, for the man he'd been before, or at least the man they had perceived him to be. Half the crowd were there for his victims. Alleged victims, perhaps, as the trial had failed to go ahead, although Shilling was loath to concede that. Standing at Florin's side, with his back to the growing throng and the uniformed officers spacing themselves carefully through the crowd, he felt like he was living through a particularly bleak Shakespearian performance. It was a Goddamn powder-keg, if ever the metaphor applied.

All things considered, Lord Pound spoke very well. Charlie watched him closely. The old man was not in the best of health. Grief had been aging him, to say the least. His turn of phrase was careful and considered. He clearly understood his audience and Shilling greatly admired the restraint and comprehension displayed. He knew that everyone was here because they had been hurt by his son, even if they had only been hurt by his loss. Harry had been a popular man, until Shilling had caught him red-handed. The women he'd killed had been popular too. Amy had been popular, well-respected, until Harry's arrest and gossip about Shilling had stripped her of that dignity.

Charlie was more than a little concerned for her. She was barely sober, and that definitely felt like his fault. He could hear her silently timing her breaths to keep herself composed. Each inhale a perfect five seconds until the exhale, and vice versa. A perfect round ten seconds. Every time. When she was called to speak, he wanted to throw himself in the way and stop her from following her father, but he couldn't bring himself to disrespect her like that, even if he thought it might be a mercy.

Florin gathered her skirts and moved with strong, regal composure to the lectern at the head of the coffin, which lay covered with wreaths and lilies. A stark, pale drop in the centre of an ocean of black umbrellas, stretching hundreds of people deep. Charlie stood and watched. She held her own umbrella neatly overhead.

Her eyes were cast down to the lectern as though there was something to read. She hadn't taken anything. He'd been watching. He couldn't look away.

He stood near her father and her friends, happy enough to be rained on by the pervasive misty drizzle, unsure quite how he had ended up in her inner circle for this. His lips pinched together as he watched her. She looked so defeated. That was wrong. Deeply and profoundly wrong. Florin shouldn't look like that. Not ever. Not her. She had a mind that could overcome anything. He had seen it in action. To see her so broken… Charlie didn't know how to fix it.

Florin sighed deeply to begin and her sigh carried across the crowd. Charlie instantly begrudged every single person there, even his own friends and family. They had no right. No right to do this to her. He thought of his own losses. No one had ever made him grieve publicly before. He did not imagine he would handle it well. She owed this crowd nothing, yet here they were to collect anyway.

"Thank you all for being here," Florin murmured, eyes resolutely downcast. "I… know that this is a difficult time for everyone, that not all of you want to be here, that… that things… that nothing about this is simple. That many of you are angry. Rightfully angry. It… it seems appropriate perhaps that the mood of Harry's funeral be one of anger, of frustration and pain… I—" she paused sharply, cutting herself off. "I don't know what to say right now… what to add to everything my father…" she trailed off and cleared her throat. "That was very well spoken before, Daddy," she muttered, finally tilting her eyes up to meet her father's. She took another deep breath, pressing her lips together for a moment before continuing. "I don't quite know how to follow that, but to agree, as we all know, Harry was a troubled man. A fool..." she trailed off softly.

Charlie watched her eyes fall on the coffin and harden. Oh no...

"No." She clipped the word out, louder and firmer than anything else she'd said since they left the house. "No. I won't be complicit in this. I am not going to pretend he was some disturbed idiot. He wasn't a fool. He wasn't stupid. If he was stupid, we would have caught him faster, we would have saved more people. He was a selfish bastard! He knew exactly what he was doing! He was a sick, perverse monster who decided he'd rather murder people than go to therapy!" She gathered her skirts again in her free hand and stormed to the coffin, glaring down at it. "You were clever, you psychotic prick! You were smart enough to know exactly what was going to happen and you—! You never slipped... you didn't, Harry. You never got sloppy. You wanted me to catch you. You knew I would eventually, and you did nothing to stop it. You forced me to do this, you bastard, and then you just up and quit on me! Get up, Harry! Get up, you unholy pile of dogshit and let me kill you myself!" She kicked the edge of the coffin with one mud-spattered boot.

"Amelia!" Lord Pound called sharply. Laura and Jane were exclaiming at his side, but Charlie moved first. He'd been waiting for it. He'd seen that look and known she was going to crack. He crossed the distance between them like it was nothing.

"Florin!" he bid her, grabbing her by the shoulders and pulling her gently back. "Come away, Florin."

She didn't move, but she stopped trying to kick Harry's coffin. She whirled on Charlie, eyes flashing dangerously beneath the dark umbrella. That was the Florin he knew. The Florin who always looked like she was prepared to kick him in the teeth if he did anything stupid. He'd missed that Florin.

"What do you want, Charlie?!" she snapped. "You want to tell me I shouldn't be angry?! That this man didn't ruin the lives of all these people?! That he didn't ruin mine?!"

"No," Charlie shook his head, still holding her shoulders. "No, Florin, funerals are for grieving. This is absolutely the time and place, but, for some reason, it is not socially acceptable. As with all things, there are completely nonsense rules and etiquette for mourning."

She stopped then, truly stopped. The fire went out of her eyes and her stance, and she looked at him that way she so often did, like she was seeing something in him that he was unaware of. It was a confusing look. However, he'd managed to pull her the inch or two far enough from the coffin that he felt comfortable letting her go. The rain was intensifying and he pushed his wet hair from his face, glancing over his shoulder at the sea of faces staring at them. He'd expected it to be horrifying, but, somehow, it didn't bother him at all. All those startled eyes, they weren't for him, and he didn't care. All those whispers and mutterings… they just made him irritable.

"Oh really?" he huffed at the crowd. "How many of you wouldn't have done exactly what she did, given half the chance? The woman just lost the love of her life twice in two months, you expect her to be okay? You expect her to stand here and perform approved gestures of grief while you gawk at her like a mourning dove in a zoo?!" He shook his head at them, gazing at the audience who seemed to have realised that he wasn't so much dashing into the rescue as throwing himself on the bonfire. "Look at yourselves, you're surrounded by uniformed supervision. How many of you came here today looking for a fight?" He realised he was yelling it like a challenge, into an audience of whom half would probably want to punch him in the face. But no one moved first. "You want to mutter and judge, but Doctor Florin is right. Everyone here is angry. Rightfully angry, because you are, all of you, victims of Harry Pound. Even his friends and family became victims of who he ended up being. I look around this crowd and all I see is a congregation of Harry's ghosts. Every single one of you has a ghost of Harry Pound that you carried here with you. But ghosts..." he paused and wiped some of the rain from his face. "Ghosts are only as real as you make them. They only haunt you if you let them. Harry is gone now. He removed himself from the story, which means everyone here gets to finish it without him. You get to choose if it's for better or worse. He no longer gets a say in how you choose to remember him or how you choose to move on. He forfeited that right." He was still speaking to the crowd when he glanced back at Florin. "This is the time and place to grieve, but it's also the time and place to walk away. What's done is done. Don't let him hurt you anymore."

Florin nodded slowly. Charlie hoped his words weren't as empty as they felt. He did mean it, but he also knew it was pointless telling people not to be hurt. It was easy for him to be logical, calculated. He'd never liked Pound Junior anyway. He hadn't been betrayed, hadn't lost anything. Not really. Not like she had. He reached back and put a comforting hand on Amy's shoulder and she let him guide her further from the coffin. He was grateful when Laura and Jane dashed out the last couple of steps to take her and pull her back in.

The minister stepped forward again, under the safety of his own umbrella, and gave Charlie an approving nod.

"Thank you, Mister Shilling," he nodded. "Very well said."

"Hardly..." Charlie muttered thickly. He reached into his jacket and pulled out the flask, taking a small sip of what was left of the awful burning liquid to clear this throat. "Harry Pound loathed me. He tried to kill me twice. If there was anything that would make him rise from the grave, it would be knowing that I was speaking at his funeral."

Shilling was very aware that he was not the only one who shot a look at the coffin after that declaration. Of course, nothing happened. Nothing was going to happen. The most exciting part of the day had already occurred. As Charlie had said, there was nothing more to do except walk away.

3

Anger was like a toxic lover. It had the power to make you feel good, justified… satisfied. Except when it left, when it wasn't there to talk you into the behaviour, the cold wake of its absence was full of shame. Amy couldn't believe she'd caused such a scene, and that Charlie had been forced to come to her rescue. Merciful God, it was so embarrassing. Her friends were being awfully kind about it. She was sitting quietly in a corner with Laura and Jane, watching the afternoon rain lash the window.

The wake was kindly being hosted by one of the Law Society clubs that Harry had belonged to, and that her father still belonged to. The old building had several meeting rooms spread across the ground floor and the mourners (if they could even be called that) were meandering and grouping through them. The rooms were all dark wood panelling with frequently spaced heavy bookshelves and many reading nooks. Amy was bundled in one currently. Drinks and cake were provided, but she was just sticking to tea for now. Taking the edge off had not, in fact, helped take any edges off.

Every time she thought about her outburst, her

temperature rose as a hot flush of mortification consumed her. Laura sat with her arm comfortingly around Amy's shoulders, holding her close while Amy quietly sipped her tea. She felt like she was trying to sober up, but wasn't really sure she was drunk to begin with. Not anymore, certainly.

"I know it doesn't feel like it," Jane said softly at her side, "but you are holding up remarkably well."

"Yes!" Laura agreed wholeheartedly. "If it were me, I'd have burnt down half of London by now."

"Can we?" Amy asked hopefully. "I really rather fancy burning down London right now."

Laura chuckled and kissed Amy's head affectionately.

"I think probably the best thing for you will be to go home and sleep this off tonight," Jane commented gently. "But perhaps tomorrow, if you're up for it, we could take you out? We could take you down to Tuppence Teahouse over in Westminster? They have the most beautiful teacakes."

"And the most beautiful tea ladies..." Laura added suggestively.

Amy chuckled weakly. "I'm not sure I can cope with beautiful tea ladies at the moment," she admitted. "I... I'm not really sure what I can cope with. I'm not sure I can rest tonight. I'm not sure I want to be alone..."

"Perhaps the Great Livre is doing a show?!" Laura suggested. "We could get you out of the house and take you to see some magic? That might be a fun distraction?"

"Perhaps a bit too much fun," Jane smiled gently.

She was looking at Amy with those knowing eyes. God, they were so knowing. "Perhaps you're after a quieter way to spend your time…?"

Amy shook her head and blushed, sipping at her tea to try and hide from the look Jane was giving her. Oh, she certainly couldn't cope with that right now.

"You know you can do better, darling," Jane murmured carefully. "I know that everything seems awful right now, but you needn't settle for—"

"Don't finish that sentence," Amy ordered. She was surprised how stern she sounded. How angry.

"She didn't mean it like that," Laura defended softly, patting Amy's knee. "We know he's your friend and that's… um… that's fine. You know, we understand. He's… of course he's… uh, well—"

"He was lovely to you at the funeral," Jane conceded. "We know there are good sides to him."

"When he's not being a rude degenerate," Laura muttered. "I'm sure in those moments he's probably perfectly reasonable. Almost cute, if you like that sort of thing. Maybe. He's a bit like a human teddy bear — obviously not one of those cute Harrods ones in uniform, but an old battered one where the fur has worn off in places and the stuffing is missing… so it's all scrawny and limp and the face is crooked…" Laura trailed off slowly as Amy gave her a death stare. Jane rolled her eyes.

"He's little and wonky, Amy, and you can do better," she insisted. "It's fine if you want to associate with him, just don't forget what you're worth. You're incredible, darling. Don't let all this make you think otherwise for a second."

Amy sat for a moment and composed herself. She wanted to explode again. She wanted to fly apart at the seams and yell at them, but they were trying to be nice. They were trying to talk her up, but they couldn't do it by talking down Charlie. Not Charlie. And the longer she let the silence reign, the more they almost seemed to realise that.

"He's incredible too," she whispered at her teacup. "I... I'm not trying to start anything, I know I can't, but please don't belittle him. He's... a good person. The best. And I... well... well, I know you two love me, and I am endlessly grateful, but let's not pretend that I am some Renaissance Venus. I am often considered less than pretty by many. Harry's friends were never short on comments regarding my size and nose and freckles and —"

"Harry's friends are scum!" Laura hissed viciously. "That doesn't count. You're beautiful."

"It doesn't matter anyway," Amy blushed furiously, "because Shilling and I are not even remotely courting in any fashion whatsoever, and I don't even know why we're having this conversation!" She cast her eyes about anxiously, but no one was paying attention to them presently muttering away in the corner. She took another deep and soothing breath, mostly to steady her nerves, and then discovered one last indignation slipping through her lips. "However," she began before she could stop herself, "I would like to point out that the raggedy bears only get that way because they are so dearly loved. It is better to be loved and worthy of love than to be beautiful and store bought."

"Amy… do you love a raggedy bear?" Jane asked.

Amy wanted to throw herself out a window, but Jane's question held far more teasing than judgement. The way her friends were watching her was almost testing, as though they wanted to see if she meant it or if she was just vulnerable. If her behaviour earlier had proven anything, she needed to be protected from herself as much as others.

"To your credit…" Laura began slowly, "he does get an awful lot of points for the way he came to your rescue out there."

"And I did need rescuing…" Amy sighed weakly. She shook her head at herself. She'd needed a lot of rescuing from Charlie since she'd found out the truth about Harry. "I feel like such a fool…" she muttered.

"I think that's normal," Jane consoled her. "But you didn't actually do anything wrong."

"I threw a tantrum and beat up a coffin," Amy reminded drily over the rim of her teacup.

"Yes, but as Shilling pointed out, who could blame you?" Laura smiled slyly. "Besides, half the people there clearly wanted to do the same thing. I think you probably made some new friends with that display." She cast her eyes across the room, catching glances from some of the other attendees.

A dangerous woman with tight curls, wearing a lavish black and red dress, caught their eye and began to approach. Amy recognised Madam Bronny. She moved with stately posture, always surrounded by a cluster of her girls. Lizzie was among them. Amy hadn't seen her since before France. Since they'd basically broken up. She wasn't sure she wanted to deal with this, but she also wasn't sure she wanted to avoid it badly enough to risk making another scene. In truth, she didn't know what she wanted.

"Our condolences, Doctor Florin," Bronny offered gently.

"For the death of Harry, my dignity, or my social standing?" Amy replied witheringly.

Bronny smiled. "Whichever grieves you most, I suppose."

Amy sighed. They were being kind to her, which meant the ignominy was her own doing.

"Thank you, Madam," she replied sincerely, taking a polite sip of tea to calm herself again. "It is appreciated."

"How are you feeling, Amy?" Lizzie asked, her face pinched with guilt.

"I've been better..." Amy admitted. She took another sip of tea, basking satisfactorily in Lizzie's guilt, until she realised she didn't want it. "But... but I've been worse too. Finding out Harry was a killer was worse than finding out he was dead... I think. Although, both have been awful."

"I can only imagine," Bronny sympathised. "All things considered, Doctor, you are holding up with admirable resilience."

"That's kind, Madam, but you don't need to—"

"I mean it," Bronny cut her off. "I know plenty of other people that would have taken to their beds and dissolved into utter reclusion in the face of tragedy like yours. Speaking of…" She cast a judgemental look at the newcomer entering their clique.

Amy smiled as Julian joined them. Black suited him and he wore it regularly, so seeing him felt less like a mourning affair. He wasn't nearly as sombre as everyone else, his handsome smile was a sight for sore eyes, and mostly she was just starting to grow fond of Charlie's sensational friend.

"Hello, Mister Silver," she greeted him.

"Amy, darling, how are you?" he inquired, pushing through and leaning over to kiss her cheek. He was hot and flushed, his stubble rough against her skin, and his thick dark curls heavily scented with soap and spices. Yes, he was definitely an easy person to be fond of.

"Mostly terrible," she smiled warmly at him. "But given the circumstances it would be strange if I wasn't."

"Aye, ain't that the truth," he agreed, straightening up and moving to stand with his old colleagues. "Beautiful show with the coffin though. I wish I'd known — I'd have brought you whisky and matches."

"I believe Lord Pound was trying to keep from starting a riot, Julian," Bronny said pointedly.

"Funerals are rubbish if there isn't at least a small riot," he replied.

Amy appreciated the sentiment, but she was also beginning to mellow into a sobriety that was grateful that they had been able to maintain a modicum of peace, if only for her father's sake. Near her, Lizzie's guilt was melting into something sly as she gave her ex-workfellow a sidelong glance.

"Julian…" she began slowly, sidling up to him.

"Lizzie?" he beamed at her, throwing an arm around her shoulders and pulling her in affectionately. She leant into it, her devious look exacerbating.

"Did I just see you sneaking out of the coat cupboard with that bookish-looking boy?" she inquired.

"Hm?" he feigned ignorance, badly.

"Oh my God, Julian..." Bronny sighed wearily, shaking her head. "The coat cupboard? Of a funeral? Really? Our overwear is in there."

"The heart wants what the heart wants, Bronny," Julian defended.

"I don't think it's your heart doing the wanting..." she muttered scathingly.

Amy watched the Madam glance across the room to eye up the allusion of Lizzie and Julian's attention. All their gazes found Michael collecting drinks from a staff member at one of the corner tables. He looked pale, unassuming, and, well, bookish, in his simple black attire — if perhaps a little rumpled. His hair looked like it had been neatly combed... before someone got their hands in it.

"So that's the boy you left us for..." Bronny commented neatly, arching an eyebrow. "Must have a cock the length of the Thames."

"Excuse me?" Julian retorted.

"Well, come now, Silver..." she goaded. "There has to be some kind of appeal, and it can't be his plain demeanour. After all, he's rather dull in appearance, isn't he?"

Amy sank back into the cushioned nook and sipped her tea protectively. Laura and Jane registered her reaction and huddled closely back with her. She wished she could throw up fortifications. This was about to get ugly. Julian was already drawing himself up like an affronted lion. Bronny seemed to realise, but it was too late to take it back.

"Are you blind?!" he demanded.

There it was. Amy tried to vanish into the upholstery. She was too close to this to afford for it to turn into another scene, and Julian was only getting started.

"Skipp is one of the most beautiful people on the planet," Julian insisted. "He's lean and cunning and graceful like a jungle cat. He has eyes like the cool azure depths of an ancient winter. He's stunning and brilliant and smarter than even Charlie. Of course he might seem humble to someone like you, but I assure you, Bronny, he's worth more than everyone in your house combined."

His anger was hardly sated, but he mellowed as Mike wandered over to join them. Amy was eternally grateful for the additional calming presence. Bronny and her girls were all still taken aback at Julian's outrage, although Lizzie's surprise was clearly tinged with amusement. Mike reached them and handed a glass to Julian.

"What are you yelling about now, love?" he asked.

"You," Julian huffed, taking the drink appreciatively.

"Oh." Mike's mild curiosity shifted instantly to dawning horror. "Julian, you promised no more public poetry."

Amy barely stifled her laughter. Her own encounters with Julian's descriptions of his lover left a lot to be desired. At least Mike knew about the truly terrible poetry. He wasn't about to get blindsided by people recounting tales of the cool depths of his eyes. Although, she made a mental note to have either Charlie or Mike let Julian know what azure actually meant at some point. She refused to engage herself for fear that she might be pulled into an impromptu workshop on synonyms for 'blue'.

Mike glanced her way as she giggled and flashed her the subtlest of winks, before nodding his head politely at her in greeting.

"Sorry for your loss, Doctor Florin. It's good to meet you properly," he held out his hand. "I've heard so much from Charlie and Julian. I'm just sorry it's not under better circumstances."

Amy unfolded herself from the depths of the corner, setting down her tea and taking Mike's hand.

"And you," she smiled. "I, likewise, have heard a great deal from the boys. Julian's descriptions of you are..." she trailed off.

"Evocative?" Mike supplied drily, cutting off any further attempts at embellishing his character.

Amy laughed appreciatively. Mike turned his introductions to the other women, shaking hands in turn with Laura and Jane before coming to Julian's old colleagues. His demeanour was so gentle and friendly Amy didn't even realise he'd been playing until he came to Madam Bronny. That was the moment she finally realised what Julian meant by 'smarter than

Charlie', which she had been quick to dismiss until she witnessed his guile in action.

"It's an honour, Madam," he shook her hand firmly. "Michael Pence, I've heard only admirable things about you."

Bronny froze mid-shake as she heard him say his name. Clearly a deliberate action on his part. He wasn't the least bit surprised by her reaction. In fact, he acted like nothing unusual was occurring at all. Nothing about his temperate nature changed. His smile didn't even slip.

"*The* Michael Pence...?" Bronny replied like she was standing off with a viper.

"I'd hardly know if it warrants an emphasis," Mike smiled. "I'm sure the name is more than common."

Bronny was staring daggers at him. Amy could see the cogs ticking behind her eyes as a great many pieces fell into place very quickly. She knew exactly who he was, and knew that he knew she knew. He'd just become infinitely more interesting, which easily explained Julian's fascination. Except Julian used to work for her, at one of the most prestigious High Houses in London, and during his time in her employ had fallen for arguably the most prolific spymaster in the city.

If Julian had been furious at Bronny's dismissal of Mike earlier, it was nothing compared to her icy rage at what was clearly unfolding before her.

"You're surprisingly unassuming, for so infamous a figure," she commented.

"You must have me mistaken for someone else,"

Mike smiled. "I'm a humble baker by trade."

"Of course you are," Bronny corrected venomously. His inconspicuous nature wasn't really surprising. It was probably the reason he was so successful. "And no doubt you dabble in a bit of this and a bit of that, here and there?"

"I couldn't have put it better myself," Mike agreed warmly. "I suppose you could say that in my downtime I have a propensity for collections and weaving..."

"And thieving," Bronny clearly couldn't help herself.

"Heavens, no," Mike smiled. "That's Julian's area."

Bronny looked like she was ready to bite. Mike seemed fully aware of this as he sipped his drink before swirling his glass, eyeing the spiralling liquid.

"For what it's worth, Madam, what you see as so treacherous a threat was actually your biggest advantage," Mike told her. "Julian was working for me much longer than you. He never betrayed you."

"I'm not sure I believe you," she countered. Her tone was cold and Amy related to it instantly. She knew exactly how that felt, except, in this instance, she was almost tempted to step in and mediate. Amy knew what betrayal felt like, real betrayal, and this wasn't it. Not by a long way. Besides, these were Charlie's boys. Maybe she was fooling herself, but if Charlie trusted someone, it was almost certainly the most efficient vetting anyone could receive.

"I care about our House, Bronny," Julian added. "And, luckily, Mike cares about me. He helped keep our nose above water when he needed to."

"And now?" Bronny asked.

"I still care," Julian shrugged.

"Now you have to ask yourself how well you trust your employees," Mike suggested carefully.

"I trust everyone I put in my house, even when I shouldn't," she countered, throwing Julian a filthy look. "Charlie warned me about you."

"Really?" Julian looked curious.

"Not in so many words…" Amy interjected. She remembered the interaction vividly. After all, it had been her introduction to Julian and the first time she'd visited a High House. There were some papers still trying to write about it, or what their delusional imaginations had concocted regarding it. Everyone looked to her, and she realised she had drawn their attention, quickly sipping her tea and breaking eye contact. The act gave her pause to consider and she pinched her lips together carefully before beginning again. "Charlie grew up in that house. He's very protective of it, so he was concerned when he realised that one of Michael's runners was working there, but I think he knew it was safe. He must have realised — in his Charlie sort of way — otherwise I imagine he would have taken steps." She met Bronny's eye. "Charlie trusts Julian, that should tell you a lot."

"And that's your entirely unbiased opinion, Doctor?" Bronny checked.

Amy flushed, though from the insinuation or how quickly everyone else jumped to her defence, she wasn't sure. There was a fast clamouring from everyone around her against the Madam. Lizzie got in more coherently than anyone else.

"That's not fair, Madam," she insisted delicately. "You know she's right. Besides, who here can actually say they have an impartial view of Charlie?"

"I would say I do…" Jane raised her hand delicately.

"No, my love, we don't," Laura chuckled. "I know you're admirably fair, and you're as good at playing Devil's advocate for Amy as you were for Harry's scummy friends, but you can't pretend that if push came to shove we wouldn't jump to his defence for Amy's sake."

Amy died inside and scrambled to cover the mess. Unfortunately, the definition of scrambling involved exacerbating mess.

"Why me?" she demanded, before being met with a host of sceptical expressions that only further inflamed her ire. "Seriously, half of you are like family to him. Why does everyone keep looking at me?"

The expressions didn't shift and it was starting to feel like they were mere seconds away from someone snickering.

"Do you actually want us to answer that?" Julian asked.

Someone snickered. Amy took the slowest and deepest sigh of her life before draining her teacup and standing. No one stopped her. They stood aside as she strode away for a refill. This time, she was going to add much needed whisky to the tea.

"Amy, wait—" Jane called after her, hurrying to follow.

She didn't stop as she heard everyone come after her.

It was easier to ignore them. Besides, she'd yet to reach the point today where she actually wanted to be around people. She wanted a moment of peace. She wanted to be left alone without people clamouring about her and offering meaningless words that changed nothing. She wanted to take Charlie and her father and maybe Laura and Jane and vacation at Argent's French estate for six to eight months until the end of the world blew over. Instead, she was just going to have to settle for a strong drink.

Charlie was beginning to dry out, but given the arid conversation available it would have been impossible not to. The wake was proving utterly tedious. Charlie had possessed no love for Harry and his friends when the entitled butcher had been alive. His death had not improved the company of his companions. Charlie was constantly avoiding conversations with overzealous opinions that seemed determined to seek him out and let him know he wasn't welcome.

The safest course of action now was to hide with Rebecca and Susan. His sisters were usually protective of him and not even the machinations of the most misogynistic of Harry's cohorts would dare take on Lady Guinea. Besides, the men quietly rubbing elbows as they genuinely grieved Pound Junior and his ideals were confident in their chauvinism, right up until they actually had to outstare Susan. Charlie was privately convinced his sister-in-law could outstare the Queen, if not Satan themself.

"Now, Charles, I understand you've been holding out on us..." Susan accosted gently, as Rebecca came over with tea and cake.

Charlie immediately stiffened with alarm, like some kind of fainting goat. Perhaps this was not so safe after all.

"Those boys you had us bring along this morning," Susan continued. "They're the same ones you've been spying on through your bedroom window. It would seem you've made some progress in that regard..."

"I daresay he has," Rebecca smirked. "Given that I just spotted the two of them sneaking out from the coat cupboard."

"Out from the where?!" Charlie startled on principle, before realising that he wasn't surprised at all and was extremely glad he'd left his coat on. "Dear God, Julian..." he muttered to himself. "Time and place, man."

"Julian Silver..." Susan pondered, carefully eating one of the dainty teacakes. "That boy looks awfully familiar... I just can't place it."

Charlie pursed his lips carefully and tried not to let his expression betray him. It was his most treacherous aspect. He had a very poor poker face. Lies might have been commonplace for humanity, but he was terrible at them.

"And he's involved with your baker friend?" Susan smiled at Charlie. "One of George Pence's boys, yes? Where does he fit in with the lads?"

"Pence siblings," Charlie corrected automatically. "It's the six Pence siblings. Michael's about in the middle. Two older, three younger. Youngest is called Harriet now."

There were long, drawn-out noises of comprehension from both his sisters as they shared a look.

"That makes so much sense," Rebecca sighed.

"It does," Susan agreed wholeheartedly. "I wonder how George felt about it."

"I believe the family were all thrilled," Charlie shrugged. "I know Mister Pence made a point of adopting the boys to work the bakery, but I think everyone feels it does them some good to have inadvertently ended up with a member of the fairer sex to help keep them rational."

"With what?" Susan exclaimed delightedly.

"It's a nonsensical gendered term used by thespians to court controversy," he sighed.

"As you tell me every time I use it," Susan smirked. "Yet here you are utilising the same phrase. I never thought I'd see the day." She eyed him rather smugly. "I note previously you never bought into the notion. Perhaps presently you may have reason to...?"

Charlie decided to try his luck outstaring Susan, but realised a good six seconds in that he wasn't going to have much success. Her dark eyes were stone cold in their resilience and no man, woman, nor child could compete.

"Bugger off..." he muttered sullenly, looking away as his cheeks began to flush.

"Now, now, Charles," she scolded him amusedly. "None of that language."

"Becky," Charlie whinged. "Your wife is teasing me."

"Someone has to, darling," Rebecca kissed his cheek affectionately.

Funerals, Charlie decided, really were the worst possible events people could be requested to attend. They were even worse than weddings. He was sure he hadn't done anything to deserve this, and was wondering what on earth he was doing here, when the reason for his attendance burst into the room with a throng of followers. Florin went straight to the bar with her teacup and requested a half-half refill. No requested halves were milk.

Charlie hadn't even realised he'd moved, but he quite suddenly found himself on his feet, approaching the crowd.

"Doctor Florin? Are you all right?" he heard himself ask, still partially wondering how he'd gotten here.

She turned to look at him and froze. All of them did. Shilling looked over the group, all of whom he was quite familiar with, and wondered what they were all staring at him for. He did, at a glance, note the rumpled conditions of Julian and Michael with mild disapproval. Really, time and place.

Before he even realised what he was doing, Charlie found himself standing at the bar with his hand resting over the top of Florin's teacup, blocking the open whisky bottle the barkeep had been set to pour. No one argued, the bottle was paused politely, but the shift of attention was growing around the room.

"You are more than entitled, Florin," he admitted. "But it would be remiss of me not to raise my concern."

She turned away from him, refusing to meet his eye and muttering exasperated and vulgar curses under her breath.

"Valid," Charlie nodded at her choice of words.

Laura and Jane closed in around Florin, standing near her as Jane rested a supportive hand on her friend's back.

"We very much appreciate that you care, Shilling," Jane told him. "But now might not be the time."

"Or the place..." Laura added, looking around the crowd turning to watch them.

Charlie glanced around and slowly took his hand back from the cup. A great many of the attendees were watching like they were expecting to get another funeral performance. He could almost see the whispered scandals hovering on strangers' lips. The notion wasn't usually one to concern him. He had grown accustomed to being the unwilling object of much gossip over the years and learnt to ignore it. However, there was Florin to consider. Even when he thought he was trying to help her avoid scandal, his mere presence was a complication. He shoved his hands in his pockets and gave a half-hearted shrug of acquiescence.

"Finally," a nasally voice drawled behind him, "someone who can actually speak his language and explain to him that he's not wanted."

"Excuse me?" Florin rounded on them.

Charlie's heart sank when he saw the trio of men perusing them over their wine glasses. LOAM — although, he was going to have to make a point of not calling them that to their faces. Not here. Not today. Just for Florin. Who looked set to do it herself.

LOAM was Charlie's acronym for the group of Harry's friends who had been petitioning for his release before his shocking death. It stood for League Of Aristocratic Misogynists, which he felt summed them up rather accurately. Although, he was certain they had a different name for themselves. He was grateful none of his acquaintances knew the members by name or face, or this might get ugly. Well, none but Florin. This had the potential to get ugly anyway.

Charlie eyed the men up quickly. The one who had spoken wasn't someone Charlie recognised. He gave off a strong energy of someone who lacked any understanding of personal space, and everything in his demeanour marked him as a sycophant showing off for the man at the back of the group. The man at the back was John Bullion and he had been one of Harry's best friends. His nearest and dearest. Old money, old blood, old associations. Despite their numerous differences in appearance, Charlie considered Harry's friends rough copies of the original. They might not be killers, but they hadn't studied the law to abide by it. Justice in their eyes was clearly considered to be a privilege for the elite: just us.

"We're not trying to be disrespectful, Amy," John placated delicately. "But this is Harry's wake. It begs the question, what is the freak doing here?"

"Honestly, John, I thought you brought him," Florin dismissed furiously, gesturing sharply at the first man beside him.

Charlie froze like a startled squirrel. He wasn't the only one. Julian had stepped forward aggressively the instant John had said the word 'freak', but Michael was holding him back by the arm and muttering in his ear. Shit! Mike would know who they were. Mike would know exactly who everyone in the room was, if anyone did. At least he might also have the sense to be careful about it.

Florin's rebound of the insult hadn't been lost on anyone. The more genteel members of the crowd froze like Charlie, and the man she'd insulted drew himself up in indignation. Bullion just smiled. It was smug and conceited and Charlie didn't like it, but mostly he didn't like it because it was concerningly cunning. Bullion placed a consoling hand on his friend's sleeve before one of them spoke in temper. Charlie feared deeply which side would crack first.

"Adam was one of Harry's friends and a friend of this club," Bullion reminded carefully. "A fact of which I am certain you are aware, Amy, although I have the utmost sympathy for the grief that must be clouding your judgement. As emotional as you are, I'm sure we both know he wasn't who I was referring to."

"Pray, then, John—" Amy began with so much venom Charlie could hear the explosion building.

"Me, Florin," he interrupted urgently before she provoked them into saying something that would cause her to start another scene. "They were talking about me."

He kept his eyes down, fidgeting with his ring so that he didn't have to look at anyone. Meeting people's eyes was bad enough when he wasn't falling on his sword. Still, he could feel the eyes on him. Not hers. Amy didn't look at him, but he could almost feel her feathers lower. The anger didn't go out of her, but it stopped rising.

"Mister Shilling was invited by my father, Lord Henry Pound," she announced proudly. "If you have anything to say on the matter, I strongly suggest you go say it to him."

"I wouldn't dream of disturbing his Lordship in his hour of grief," Bullion replied carefully. "Of course he is more than entitled to invite anyone he wants. In fact, he showed great wisdom in his invitation to the vast spread of law enforcement on this dark day. I'm sure Shilling was merely caught up in the net of appeasement to the rabble."

"Of course, with such an appeasement met," the third man finally joined the conversation haughtily, "you'd think 'the smartest man alive' would also be able to deduce when he's not wanted..."

"Maybe he's not that smart," Adam snickered.

"Maybe he's not unwanted..." Bullion suggested damningly, staring at Amy like a fox cornering a rabbit. "It's funny, Amy, Harry always spoke so highly of you. The way he talked marked a reverence greater than that of Aphrodite or Athena — but they've been writing some very interesting things about you recently..."

"Believed by fools and coveted by perverts," Charlie

snapped, stepping between them, straight into the line of fire. "The gossipmongering to which you allude has already been disproven as libel. No one who actually knows the Pounds or Doctor Florin believes it, a fact of which I am certain you are aware, Bullion. Painfully, I have noted the gross degeneration of character in those who choose to humour it, although I have the utmost sympathy for the grief that must be clouding your judgement. As emotional as you are, I'm sure we both know the fiction is only concocted to appeal to the lowest morality, in an effort to boost sales of a filthy rag preferred by those of an inferior intellect."

Bullion swirled the wine in the bottom of his glass and sipped it gently, all but ignoring the way Charlie used his own words against him. His friends had grimaced. Lord Bullion's son didn't.

"God, Shilling," he commented disparagingly. "There's no need to get hysterical about it."

Bullion's friends laughed, casting each other appreciative glances.

"You can't blame the freak, John," Adam simpered. "Everyone knows he's prone to female hysteria."

"Prone to what?" Bronny demanded, adjusting her stance at his shoulder.

Everyone in Shilling and Florin's company shifted their weight at the claim, drawing tighter around the narcissistic men. For the first time since they had started, the LOAM boys seemed to realise they might be in trouble. Madame Bronny was a formidable woman in her own right. With a small cluster of her girls, and Julian and Mike, plus Florin and her fellow doctors, with Susan and Rebecca Guinea on Charlie's other side, it was an intimidating sight, to be sure. Charlie almost didn't want to watch. Almost.

"It's a documented condition," the third man defended, doubling down despite the encroaching air of violence.

"So's possession by unearthly entities," Jane scoffed.

"So's male bluster driven by inadequate phallic size," Laura smirked. "I believe they stem from the same school of thought, despite a profound lack of recorded evidence by any medical institution. Although, present conversation does make me wonder if an investigation is warranted." She finished by eyeballing him with devastating deliberation.

Julian and several of Bronny's girls laughed. The LOAM boys flushed. Even Bullion was looking flustered, realising they were outnumbered, as his friends began to lose their cool.

"What would two carpet-munching sluts know about anything," Adam snapped.

The air went out of the room, turning it cold and stale. Even Bullion closed his eyes with a pained grimace. As much as he might've agreed with the sentiment, he was smart enough to recognise when the first punch was thrown, and it had been by his side. Charlie was trying to fathom if he was going to stoop to their level, or just grab a shovel and go for it, when Susan made her presence felt.

"I believe, Mister Indium, that Doctors Mark and Franc know a good deal more about legitimate and phoney medical conditions than an incomplete business education would have instilled in you. Especially given that it seems to have done nothing to improve your character and everything to deteriorate your manners." She spoke with a cutting edge reminiscent of being scolded by one's mother, and an underlying threat that said actual mother would be informed of the transgressions.

"I hardly need schooling from you, Guinea," Adam snapped stupidly.

Charlie removed himself from the situation. No one was paying him any attention anymore, and it was probably safer and more effective if he didn't involve himself. Besides, if he had to stay there and listen to anymore vulgar bigotry drip from those mouths, he was liable to end up hiding more bodies in Harry's coffin.

Safely out of the room, he ducked away and leant against the corridor stairs with a deep and soothing breath. He stimmed the buttons of his coat, running his finger around and around the cold smooth surface. No one else was out here and he could take a moment to calm himself, away from prying eyes.

Men like that were the reason he loathed the aristocracy. Well, one of the reasons. The entitlement and injustice they could wield, subjugating millions of people who either didn't agree with them or didn't fit their ideals in other ways, lit a fire of anguish in Charlie that made him want to raze society. Choking back the flames every day was exhausting. Caustic. The only way to survive it was to disengage, focus on work, and slowly but surely chip away at the system.

That was the sensible reaction. At least he was still in a position to make it. When the anger hit it was so toxic it rendered him irrational. Still, despite the homicidal urges, he knew he didn't have it in him to kill anyone. Not really. Besides, what did it solve? They'd just buried Harry Pound and nothing was better. None of the women he'd killed had been revived. Their families and friends were no less traumatised. Pound Senior and Doctor Florin were complete messes. Harry's friends were still the human equivalent of sloppy dog turds and bragging about it.

Nothing changed.

It was suffocating.

Charlie started as a hand rested on his shoulder. He hadn't heard the footsteps over the blood pounding in his ears. He hadn't noticed the perfume after acclimatising to the scent in his own hair. He should have realised.

"Charlie…?" she inquired. "Are you okay?"

"Fine, Florin," he nodded, sighing apologetically. "Sorry. I thought it safer to extricate myself."

"You are not the one who needs to be apologising," Florin insisted. "Although, I imagine the others are deep in the process of wresting one now."

"I suppose we should be helping," he muttered.

Florin shrugged. "I've never seen a dumb chicken get ripped apart by a pack of wolves and I'm not prepared to start here. If John and his friends want to get eviscerated by Madame Bronny and Lady Guinea, that's their business. It's probably the most exciting female attention they've had all year, even if it does end up qualifying as a hate crime."

"Indeed," Charlie grimaced. "Better to stay away. Besides, if I had to watch the evisceration, I might be prone to a bout of female hysteria..."

Florin slapped his shoulder, but she grinned at his impertinence. That was all it took. The pressure lifted and he smiled, casting his eyes down and fidgeting with his ring. The metal was smooth and slippery against his finger, turning effortlessly with familiar and practiced ease. It was comforting, but maybe just habit too. He couldn't bring himself to stop, even if the impulse was becoming more stressful than soothing. He didn't want to be fidgeting in her company. She was half the relief. That he had made her smile, even here and now, that was reassuringly pleasant.

"Florin... I—" he began hesitantly, dismayed that he couldn't bring himself to meet her eye.

"Oi! Shilling!" a gruff voice called down the hallway.

Shilling and Florin both turned to see two uniforms striding their way. Charlie recognised Constables Wilson and Bond heading towards them.

"Oh God, what did I do now?" he huffed, shoving his hands irritably into the pockets of his coat.

"I dunno..." Wilson eyed him cautiously. The two officers slowed as they neared them. "What did you do?"

"And is it something we should know about?" Bond added, eyeballing him.

"You just called out to me," Charlie reminded them exasperatedly.

"Yeah," Wilson agreed, clearly confused as to how

the two things were connected. "We've got a case."

"We need your help," Bond added politely. "If you're not busy doing other things, and if those things aren't things we need to know about."

Charlie squinted at them like they were mad. They returned the look in kind. He remembered the officers as artfully obtuse, but this was a new level of discombobulation. Florin stepped between them, hands apart, guiding them back. She had a sympathetic smile on her face as she glanced at both sides.

"Mister Shilling has been suffering a rather trying day and I imagine he would welcome the distraction of a case," she interjected carefully.

"It's a tricky one," Wilson frowned. "Locked room mystery. That's your tea and biscuits, isn't it?"

"There's a missing girl," Bond informed them. "Her parents said they wanted you specifically. Supposedly they're your friends?"

"I have friends?" Charlie raised an eyebrow.

"Oh Charlie…" Florin sighed, laying a hand on his shoulder. He realised what he'd said as he glanced to her.

"You have children?!" The words were preposterous before they came out of his mouth, but his brain was starting to feel like soup. The look she gave him was deservingly derivative. "Mike and Julian have children…?"

Florin ignored him and turned with patient inquisition to the officers.

"Lord and Lady Gallium," Bond elaborated.

"The Galliums are Susan's friends—" Charlie began

dismissively before stopping short. "Esther's missing?"

Wilson and Bond nodded.

"You know her?" Florin checked.

"Delightful child," Charlie replied, his brain rebooting fully as titbits of fact filtered through his mind at speed. "Encouragingly literate." He was tapping his finger against one of his buttons at the same speed as his thoughts, barely registering the vibrations.

Locked room. Missing girl. Obedient child. Not the kind to rebel. Wealthy family. Safe environment. Careful parents. Respectable parents. Not overwhelming. Good people, wouldn't be close with Susan if they weren't. Old house though. Very old. Esther only eleven. Twelve at most. Maybe twelve. Tricky age. Could be tricky. Sneaking out? No. Why the locked room?

He stopped tapping the button and looked the officers in the eye.

"Take me to look," he ordered. "Tell me what you know on the way."

They nodded and turned to lead on. He strode after them, finally cognisant enough to notice his surroundings. There was a loud bustle of skirts at his side.

"Florin?" he inquired curiously as she strode along just behind him.

"You're not bloody leaving me here," she muttered, hooking her arm around his elbow.

SHILLING & FLORIN BOOK THREE

4

The ride to the Galliums was painfully uncomfortable. It shouldn't have been, but every trip in a police carriage felt like being arrested to Charlie. Having Florin there helped, but in a strangely unhelpful way. The pressure of where they had just left and how the morning had gone was an oppressive weight, and the constables were more awkward than he was. Not that he was ever one to complain about a lack of small-talk, but the looks the two officers kept shooting each other and the little noises they made and the sheer, unrelenting discomfort of everyone pretending like everything was fine was driving him mad.

Finally, after one awkward look too many, and twenty minutes of socially inept 'did somebody die' energy, Shilling cracked.

"Yes, actually," he muttered to them. "Someone did die."

It was a simple answer to the unspoken question of uncomfortable silence, especially given that they had been collected from a wake, but apparently it wasn't taken that way. Florin covered her mouth with a hand, but Charlie could see her smiling. All things considered, he had no idea what she was smiling about. Then, even worse, the hidden smile dissolved into soft laughter. The instant she started, the police began to join her, and Shilling was left to stare around them all in complete bewilderment.

Everyone in the world was insane except him.

Even his beloved Amy. It made no sense. Although, there was a little bit of him that didn't need it to make sense. It was nice just to see her smile. After this morning, perhaps a bit of insanity was allowed. She seemed to realise the madness, or she simply read his confusion.

"I'm so sorry," she apologised, still trying not to laugh. The mirth in her eyes was beautiful.

"I don't get the joke," he admitted.

Wilson and Bond laughed harder. Charlie glowered. Amy smiled at him. She smiled at him so beautifully his chest ached and he wished they had stayed on the boat from France and never come home. He wished he was back at the railing with her there, finally at peace with their relationship, and accepting of his own affection for her without the pressure everyone in London kept placing on them. He wished for somewhere that they could walk among the trees and talk of books and theatre and things that were not so horrible as death.

But wishes were for fools, and reality was tangible. There was no point wishing for things that could be when reality already was. The discomfort of the previous silence had been broken by everyone else's laughter. Even if Charlie was still befuddled by it.

"Did you hear back about the book?" he asked, knowing that she'd sent the manuscript off. He was the one who had told her she should. He'd insisted she do something to distract from his investigation of Harry's death. It had seemed the best option, and she had agreed — although perhaps just to appease him.

She didn't reply. At least, not in words. Her hand had folded over, even though she was still covering her mouth, and her fingers were curled and hidden by her lips. The smile wasn't gone yet, and there was a brand new layer to it. A depth of repressed delight that answered his question, even if she wasn't prepared to give voice to it yet.

He smiled back, pleased for her, and probably a touch smug, if he was being honest. He had been insistent that it was good enough. With that small victory, and something of the hideousness of the wake washed away, he turned his attention to the rolling cityscape out the window and tried to ignore the strange police officers and their cumbersome silence.

Charlie was an interesting person to watch, Amy found. It was almost as though she could see his thoughts as they appeared across his face, like a book written in an undiscovered language. She was starting to learn to read it, starting to learn to translate it. Watching the ever so slight variation in degrees at which he cocked his head, the creases that flickered sporadically across his brow, the thinness that pinched his lopsided frown, the tightness around his grey eyes... even the various tics and fidgets of his fingers as they moved from his ring to his buttons to his hair to his pockets, and every other order therein, was becoming a fascinating study. Even a rather joyous hobby.

It didn't matter that everyone had started to notice that she did it. She didn't care that Harry's friends were scathing. They weren't worth her energy anyway. They weren't worth half of him. Despite their money and influence, Charlie was so much smarter and more observant than they were, and it was interesting to look at the world like he did. It was interesting to look at him under the same lens by which he observed reality. It was also useful.

So far, she'd used it to catch a serial killer, discover her birth parents, and very recently mediate between Charlie and the police. For all that he could be brilliant, he could also be stubborn, and recently he'd been more of a mess than usual. People didn't seem to understand that Charlie was fragile. They saw the scruffy defiance and missed the emotional intensity behind his subtle tics. The immediate misunderstanding between him and the law, two parties who were already prepared to throw down in a gutter on any given day, had been escalating quickly before she stepped in. Over a stupid turn of phrase, no less. Bless them.

Constables Wilson and Bond had escorted them politely to the Galliums' residence. Amy didn't know Abraham and Constance well, but they had met a few times at parties and events. This evening they were understandably much paler and more strained than she remembered. They were glad to see Charlie though. The immediate relief to see Shilling at their door, to know that he had come when they had called, Amy could relate. She imagined that if she had lost someone, knowing Shilling was looking for them would be hugely comforting.

That was, until the questions started.

Charlie and Amy stood in Esther's room, surveying the scene, while Wilson and Bond waited with the Galliums in the doorway. Everyone was watching Charlie and Charlie was watching the room, head cocked, brows furrowed. She could see the cogs of his mind whirling like a cyclone behind stormy grey eyes and wondered what he was thinking. The first words out of his mouth were ponderous, but cutting enough to feel like a direct question.

"Why the locked room?" he asked, stepping up to Esther's desk and gently leafing through the open diary. They'd been told about the diary. Wilson and Bond knew about the runaway letter contained within. The parents didn't believe it. Besides, the bedroom had been locked. She shouldn't have been able to leave.

Amy wasn't surprised that was his first question. It wasn't just a locked bedroom door. This wasn't just privacy. The windows were padlocked. Just looking around it was a gut-chilling reminder of the beautiful prison Argent had kept her mother in at his estate in France.

"For her safety," Abraham answered. "She's a somnambulist. The maids and I, even her mother, would find her out in the corridors at night banging about. We installed the locks as she got older, for fear that she would hurt herself trying to escape the room in her sleep."

"We've seen doctors, priests…" Constance murmured tearfully. "She said the room was haunted. We had it exorcized, but—"

"Charlie!" Amy rebuked him, as he rolled his eyes at the traumatised woman.

"It was our money to spend, Mister Shilling," Abraham reminded, although his tone suggested he shared some sympathy for the scepticism. "Esther wasn't wholly wrong. There were strange noises, strange smells, strange energies and such in the room… there are some things in this world that can't be accounted for. Unfortunately, none of our attempts to cleanse the space seemed to change anything, and her sleepwalking has been a lifelong condition."

"Lifelong?" Amy arched an eyebrow.

"Since she was a small child," Abraham admitted. "We thought the locks would help keep her safe from trips and falls and any dangerous items within the house or — God forbid — if she made it outside."

"Studies have shown somnambulism is more prevalent in children," Amy mused. "There's a chance she'll grow out of it. Does she have any other parasomnias or psychological disorders?"

"What is that supposed to mean?" Constance demanded.

"Nothing so prevalent that it has been diagnosed," Abraham answered. "Her doctors have also mentioned that she may grow out of it. They said it could be hereditary. My mother was a somnambulist in her youth."

"Medically fascinating, but irrelevant," Charlie commented, crouching by the windows to inspect the latches. "Whoever took Esther doesn't know about the somnambulism."

"Whoever took her?!" Abraham echoed.

Charlie gave him a withering look. "You didn't call me here because you thought she'd genuinely run away."

"But… but the letter!" Constance protested.

"Is obviously a fake," Charlie replied. "Even the constables worked that much out."

In the doorway, Bond gave Wilson a cheeky elbow and a sly look, like they knew they'd done well.

"No…" Charlie sighed, moving along the wall with his ear pressed to the wallpaper. "Someone else was here. Someone who took Esther while she was sleeping and tidied up afterwards to hide the evidence. Someone who didn't know the room was locked when they left a note to say she'd run away…" He knocked on the wall but it gave only the low thud of brick beyond the panelling. "Constables, would you please take the Galliums downstairs and have them comprise a list of anyone who might want to take Esther or target the family in any way?"

"We already did that yesterday," Bond replied. "When we worked out the note was fake."

"We're not stupid," Wilson added. "This is actually our job and we do know what we're doing."

Charlie turned and gave them a surprised look. While Amy found it adorable, she was certain it wasn't helping.

"Any notable leads?" she asked, before he started another fight with the officers.

"We wouldn't have come to him if there were," Wilson admitted. "We know the room was locked up tight and that the note was written by someone else. That's a Shilling kinda problem, and the Galliums here said you'd help."

"Esther likes you, Charles," Abraham implored. "She always speaks well of you."

"Her opinion of me is irrelevant to my locating her," Charlie commented, his attention once again absorbed by the wall.

Amy was starting to remember why she had once found him annoying. True, there were now occasions where she found his lack of social proficiency endearing, but occasions like this were just painful. These people were suffering the worst nightmare a parent could fathom, and Charlie responded to it with all the compassion of a dead duck. Still, as hard as it was to watch him interact with their concerns, she knew his dismissal wasn't a lack of empathy. If anything, it suggested the opposite.

"Perhaps," she began, turning to the congregation in the doorway, "you could gather the servants somewhere downstairs? He may want to speak to anyone else who might have been in the house that night. I'm sure you've already taken the liberty, Officers, but you know Charlie. He'll have his own questions."

"Of course, Doctor," Abraham nodded.

"Anything to help find Esther," Constance agreed.

Bond gave Wilson a nudge. "I'll take these two down to start wrangling people. You watch shifty and our good doctor."

"Yup," Wilson nodded.

Bond escorted the Galliums away as Charlie began moving the small bookcase near the desk and checking down behind it.

Florin left him to it and picked up the diary. It was worth investigating herself. Sure enough, the handwriting of the new note didn't match the old entries. It tried. Someone had attempted to copy little Esther's script, but it was a poor imitation at best. Sloppy work, really.

Charlie's investigation moved on from the walls as Florin flicked through the diary. It felt improper to read it, but if there were any clues that would help them find her, that would make it worth it. A significant number of entries were dedicated to one of Esther's classmates. A boy called Timothy who was described as both pleasant of manner and gentle on the eyes. Florin smiled discreetly to herself as she read. The girl's vocabulary was very good. Charlie had described her as encouragingly literate. The slim diary sat lightly in her gloved hands. It was bound in pale green fabric, with a satin ribbon for a bookmark. More than half of it was ratty with use and clearly well-loved.

Last week, there was an entry about fighting with her mother. Esther's riding lessons would be cancelled unless her numeracy grades improved, and she would not be getting a new pony. It was the end of the world.

Her parents were the worst people to ever exist and had never done anything good for her. Amy turned the page. She recalled a similar argument she'd had with her father once when she'd been about the same age. It didn't warrant further investigation.

Another entry from five weeks ago made her stop and read carefully again. She shouldn't be looking, but she couldn't help it. It wasn't relevant. It wasn't important. It was, however, entertaining. Apparently, Lady Guinea and her family had come for dinner. Amy made a small mental pocket in the back of her mind where she safely tucked away the description of Shilling as a darling man, both attractive and shrewd, who was clearly far too clever to be forced to sit through small talk with monotonous company. Though obviously bored, he was full of patience, his countenance as kind as his smile, which brought a sparkle to his eyes. Oh goodness, Esther was even going to look into taking up pottery.

Amy put a hand over her mouth to stop herself from laughing. At least she had company in her admiration of Charlie, even if it was just one girl's prepubescent crush. It was nice to see someone else had noticed he was, in fact, a darling man. And Esther hadn't even seen him half-dressed and covered in clay. Amy turned the page again. Her lips were already pressed together as tightly as they would go, and if she didn't stop looking at the note she would definitely start laughing.

Charlie had moved on to an inspection of the bed, carefully peeling the sheets back and delicately sniffing the pillows.

"Oi!" Wilson snapped at him. "What do you think you're doing?"

"Trying to discern who might have taken Esther from her bed," Charlie replied.

"And that means sniffing the bed like a pervert, does it?" Wilson interrogated.

Charlie all but ignored him. He ran his olfactory sense along the crisp edge of folded sheet where the kidnapper's hands would had to have set the bedclothes neatly back.

"The able human body is home to five core senses, Constable," he murmured, standing straight again. "It would be a shame to only use as few as you do."

Amy tried to shoot him a warning look, but he was busy pulling the bed out from against the wall — or trying to.

"You find anything useful in the diary, Florin?" Charlie puffed, barely scraping the heavy wooden frame a few inches across the floor. Wilson let him struggle for a moment before coming to help.

"Only the letter," Amy signed. "It's the only thing that even so much as hints that something's afoot."

"What do you make of it?" Charlie grunted, using Wilson's help to haul the bed into the centre of the room.

"Clearly a fake," she shrugged. "And a rather sloppy one at that." She paused as she flicked back to it and looked it over again. "You... you don't think perhaps it's real, do you?"

Charlie stood and straightened his clothes, pushing his hair back from his eyes and looking to her.

"It's real in that you're holding it," he pointed out.

"Yes, thank you," she smiled. He really was on form today. "I mean you don't think perhaps there might be some sincerity to it? She might not have written the letter herself, but perhaps she did run away with the writer?"

"Then why not write it herself?" Charlie asked, moving to the wall behind the bed and continuing his investigation along the skirting boards.

"All manner of reasons, I'm sure," Amy replied. "Why don't you find her and ask her?"

Charlie smiled at her snark. He leant against the wall again and began to knock.

"What is it about the letter that makes you think she might have been involved?" he asked.

Amy pursed her lips as she thought. Charlie banged on the wall. It made a shockingly hollow sound. Amy's eyes shot up. There was nothing obvious or different about that section of the wall, save for the noise, but it had all their attention. Shilling grinned at it, full of cunning satisfaction.

Wilson moved back to the doorway and whistled for Bond, yelling for someone to find his partner and send them back up.

"Florin?" Charlie queried as he felt around the wall.

"Hm?" she replied, absorbed in his discovery.

"The letter?" he repeated.

"Oh, um..." she dropped her eyes to the diary again. "Well, it's..." She looked it over carefully. "It's a weak effort, isn't it? Someone made an attempt at Esther's handwriting, but it wasn't a good attempt. It certainly doesn't speak to any kind of professionalism. Besides, all it says is she fought with her parents and ran away. If that's a fabrication, it's a soft one. If someone was kidnapping Esther with dangerous intentions, why not embellish things to incriminate the parents? Surely that would keep any investigation away from the perpetrator for longer. Unless it was the parents… but in that case, why ask for you? Why not pretend the room wasn't locked and just tell everyone she ran away?"

"The same thought had occurred to me," Charlie admitted. "It wasn't her parents. Their confusion and distress is genuine. Besides, someone else was in here."

"Then, perhaps, she did fight with her parents, and if someone had enticed her to run away and scrawled a note…"

"Enticed?" Wilson raised an eyebrow at her.

Amy snapped the diary shut and waved it with gentle insinuation in his direction.

"She appears to be of an age where she has boys on her mind," she admitted.

"Any in particular?" Charlie asked.

"A couple," Amy confessed. "But believe me, just because she's writing about them doesn't mean they know she exists. I'd be more interested in making sure none of the help have sons her age who also happen to have gone missing."

"You think she takes after you then?" Wilson eyed her.

"How on earth is that taking after me?!" Amy demanded.

Wilson shot a look at Shilling's back. It was less than a second, but it carried weight. If the officer hadn't been half the room away, Amy would have slapped him for it. At least Charlie hadn't noticed, and no one else was around to have seen it.

They were all saved from further aggravation by a small click followed by a louder clunk. A panel of the wall, which had not previously been notable, pushed in and began to roll aside on quiet runners. Charlie stood in the new, dark and dusty doorway, silhouetted by cobwebs.

A shuffle of hurried footsteps announced Constable Bond arriving in the other corridor. As soon as the officer made it to the doorway a loud and profane exclamation was raised.

"Yeah, there's a bit of that," Wilson agreed.

All four of them stared at the secret passage. The light from Esther's bedroom illuminated the beginning of a tight spiral staircase down into the darkness. Shilling was the closest and the first to draw his sleeve across his face. The smell hit Amy next, and she immediately pulled a handkerchief from her pocket and held it to her nose. Apparently, the staircase led beyond the basement to the sewers under London. Of course it did.

"That explains the noises and the smells," Charlie commented. "And it very much solves our locked room mystery."

"How'd you know that was there?" Wilson demanded.

"A surprising number of these old houses have

hidden passages and escape routes," Charlie replied. "Susan's house has two of them."

"What's the bet you found them the first week you moved in?" Bond teased.

"I was curious," Charlie shrugged. "They're not so tricky, if you know what you're looking for."

"I'm guessing the Galliums don't know about this…" Amy muttered.

Charlie turned to face the officers watching him.

"One of you bring a torch and follow me," he insisted. "The other call for backup and get this room cordoned off. It's officially a crime scene."

"Who do you think you are?" Wilson demanded.

"Yeah, that's our job," Bond added. "You think you're going first?"

"You don't get to fire him just because he found the next clue," Amy interceded. "Charlie got hired for this case because the police were stumped. Do what I do and be grateful he's letting you tag along at all."

She turned to follow after him but paused as she reached his shoulder. He wasn't moving. The Charlie she knew was liable to charge on ahead and throw himself into danger whenever the opportunity presented itself. A faint memory stirred in the back of her mind. Something she'd gotten so used to that she'd almost forgotten it. Underground. Charlie never used the Underground. He could cope with basements, she thought, but tunnels under the city…

"Charlie…?" she touched his shoulder and he jumped slightly, ripping his eyes from the dark staircase to look at her. There was something in his eyes she'd never seen before. Not like this. This wasn't perfectly logical and rational fear, the likes of which he was so often dangerously immune. This was phobia. He was terrified. Very silently and stoically terrified.

"Hm," he replied to her, and the sound was painfully strained. "Perhaps it is a bit haunted..." He shook himself lightly and looked over his shoulder at the officers. "Anyone else feel someone walking over their grave?"

"If you're too chicken shit, we can take it from here," Wilson offered.

"We're here to find a kid, not start a fight," Bond mediated, collecting a small lantern and lighting it. "You go radio this in and get us more uniforms. Keep the Galliums away. I'll take the sleuths down to stinktown and see if his sensitive wee nose can sniff out more clues down there."

No one argued with her and Amy was grateful Bond had taken charge the way she did. It saved them anymore posturing. She fell in step with the officer, taking the lead down into the darkness. Charlie followed close behind, but Amy could hear the hesitation in his steps behind them. She reached back and took his hand. In her head, it was to reassure him and keep him close, but the further down they went the more she wondered if she was reassuring herself.

The stone staircase was dusty and tight. The light from Bond's lantern was partially blocked by her shadow, and the darkness felt thick and cloying. The smell only got worse as they travelled deeper. Raw sewage and rot... it took all Amy's strength not to upend her lunch. She drew her handkerchief from her pocket and held it to her face with one hand, the other keeping hold of Charlie. The rushing of water echoed off the tunnels beneath and bounced back up the staircase. They were definitely heading down into the sewers.

She could hear Charlie's breath becoming ragged behind her and his hand tightening painfully on hers. It was not the kind of air you wanted to be hyperventilating. She squeezed his hand comfortingly. He didn't squeeze back.

"You're going to be okay, Charlie," she promised, whispering back to him.

"You don't think Wilson was right then?" he muttered hoarsely.

Amy squinted in the dark. She remembered with a flicker of rage the look the constable had shot at Charlie just before he'd opened the secret passage. The way Wilson's eyes and tone had implied that Charlie was lesser, even while he solved the puzzle in front of them.

"No," she replied. "No, Charlie, I don't. I know this is a bad time. I know you're working, and a girl is missing, and we've spent all day at that miserable funeral, and I'm dragging you into the last place on earth you want to go… but you're good at this. You're the best at this. You solved the locked room mystery in ten minutes, when no one else had! That's why the Galliums requested you, it's why everyone else is so bitter and nasty to you. They're just jealous, Charlie. Don't let them bully you." She wasn't sure if her hushed whispers were getting lost in the growing noise of rushing water. He was silent in response. Allowing him to hear her while keeping their conversation private was a fine line to tread.

"What…?" he finally muttered. The confusion in his voice was strangely comforting. "Florin… are you… are you upset with me?"

"No, Charlie," she smiled, and held her handkerchief to her face again for a moment, steeling herself against the stench. "I'm not mad at you. Not at all. But you shouldn't let anyone else get in your head. Don't let them call you names or imply you're not good enough. You are."

He was silent again for a long time. She hoped the lengthy pauses were consideration of her words and not just inescapable terror at their situation. When he did speak, his breath was by her ear and the warmth of it was startling.

"Florin, is this about Bullion and his cronies at the wake?" Charlie whispered.

She pinched her lips a moment. It wasn't supposed to be, but she wasn't going to fool herself into believing that wasn't still bothering her.

"You shouldn't have conceded that freak comment to them," she whispered, turning her face closer to his.

He blinked at her. He was so close in the faint, partial light, washed out and pale in his black clothes with the gothic backdrop, like some kind of ghost. But those eyes. God, those grey eyes. You could just get lost in them.

Amy slipped. Her polished shoe caught the uneven stone of the stairs and shot out. Her cry was cut short by the stop. She didn't fall. She felt like she was staring down into an abyss of darkness, but Bond's head poked around the bend and she shone her lantern back.

"You two okay?" she asked. "Careful. It's getting a bit slippery down here." She stood and waited, holding the light up between them so that the stairs were clearly visible for them to cross.

Amy risked a look back. She could feel Charlie's hand gripping hers tightly, holding her upright and stopping her from falling. Her eyes traced along the collar of his shirt, at the level she stood, another step below him. Her heart was hammering everywhere. She could feel her pulse raging in her throat and her fingers. Her entire torso throbbed with her heartbeat, like it had affected her lungs. It probably had. She was just startled. Quite startled. She didn't even notice Charlie's other hand holding her waist until he let her go.

"We're all right, thank you, Constable," he announced. "The path is a little treacherous for funeral attire, but it's too late to turn back now. Good thing I already had hold of you, Florin."

Amy's heartbeat was taking up too much space in her oesophagus to reply, even when Bond's eyebrows did something she intensely resented. They crossed the steps to join the officer carefully, and she kept a tight hold of Charlie's hand the whole way. At least he didn't seem to be panicking anymore.

"We're nearly at the bottom, I think," Bond consoled them as they reached her, and she moved her light back to the staircase in front of her.

The echoes of the passage and the sewer pressed in

tightly as they wound further down, but the constable was right. Amy was mostly calm again as the end of the passage came into view. Bond stopped at the bottom of the stairs. It opened out onto a railed walkway with a view of the open sewer. She paused and looked back at them, holding her lantern up to illuminate their faces.

"Gotta say, Mister Shilling, I'd have to be feeling pretty desperate to run away through here," she commented.

"This is a perfectly functional escape route, Constable," Charlie replied. His tone was calm and even. Amy appreciated it, until she realised the trembling she felt in her fingers wasn't hers. His quivering grip in her hand was the only clue she had to his state of mind. "I'm sure there are many reasons one would choose to use it. However, I'm inclined to agree that Esther did not come this way by choice. There were too many signs that someone else was in her room."

Amy wanted to ask him what he meant, but this was what he did, and if nothing else there was the letter in the diary clearly scrawled by another hand.

"So, what are we looking for, Shilling?" Bond asked, shining her lantern across the ground. "Scuffed boot prints? Pipe ash? Torn fabric?"

"You jest, Constable, but you are also correct and you know it," he replied. "We are looking for evidence that someone had been through here and which way they went. This is basic police work and investigation practice."

He let go of Amy's hand to crouch down and inspect the ground near where Bond was holding her lantern.

Amy got a clear view of the officer's grin as she watched him do it. She wondered if the cops enjoyed getting Shilling to do their jobs for them, or if it was just fun to tease him should they reach the point that his expertise was required.

Amy covered her nose and mouth with the handkerchief again as she tried to breathe. Her eyes were adjusting to the dimness and she peered through the darkness curiously. Bond's lamplight glinted off the edges of the surrounding surfaces, marking the other side of the tunnel, the dripping trickles along the walls, the river flowing beneath them, even the endless rails marking the walkways in both directions. Dark spots of inky blackness along the walls marked alcoves spaced evenly through the tunnel. Amy squinted through the darkness, a horrible silhouette catching her eye.

Charlie was still crouched down, making sure no shred of evidence went undiscovered. Amy stood between him and the object of her growing horror. She reached silently for Bond's hand, moving her lantern.

"What are you—?" Bond began.

"Florin! I still need that!" Charlie protested.

Amy put her other hand out to keep him still, positioning herself so that there was no chance he could see past her skirts. There was the fraction of a second of inhalation as the light fell. Bond screamed first. Her shriek echoed terrifyingly off the walls. She stuck her head back into the staircase and bellowed for her partner, the call reverberating deafeningly all the way up. Amy still held her by the wrist. She adopted her best doctor's authority with a short sharp command.

"Take Charlie back upstairs and send Wilson down," she ordered.

"You take him up!" Bond yelled. "This is a crime scene!"

Esther's naked body was hanging bloody and mangled from the ceiling. Someone had strung a rope, and from this angle it looked as though she'd been mounted on a hook. The body wasn't bleeding anymore, but the dark pool beneath it was telling. It turned slightly, exposing the Glasgow smile and missing eyes, as well as more of the carved flesh on her chest and the message cut into her torso.

Hello

Shilling

Charlie was standing, pushing between them before either of them could stop him.

"Charlie, no—!" Amy tried to grab at him, but he shoved through. She glimpsed his face in the half-light. He looked dead. Something in his eyes had gone out and his skin looked grey.

"Get her down..." he muttered. "Why aren't you getting her down...?"

"Mister Shilling, this is a crime scene," Bond reminded sharply. Hurried footsteps were echoing down the staircase towards them. "Wilson! Keep the Galliums away! We need officers!" she yelled. The constable looked torn between trying to manage what might be on the stairs and the two civilians-turned-detectives panicking with her. Amy went for the lantern, but Bond shoved her off.

"Mister Shilling!" Bond yelled.

Charlie shrugged out of his coat, wrapping it around the dead girl and struggling to lift her off the hook.

"Get her down!" Charlie cried. "You can't leave her like this!"

"Christ, Shilling! Don't tamper with the evidence!" Bond shrieked. "You always say that!"

The light flashed across his face. Amy wasn't sure where her heart was, but she felt it flicker like it was about to stop. His crooked face was slack like melted stone and his eyes clouded like fogged glass. Charlie wasn't home.

5

The morgue was worse than normal. Everything was worse than normal. Amy's hands were still trembling and she couldn't get them to stop. It was late, so late that maybe it was early. She needed to eat and sleep, but she didn't feel like doing either. She couldn't leave here, not until the job was done. She might not have been able to do the work herself, but she wasn't going to let anyone else do it unsupervised. Not with the way everyone was treating Charlie.

Exacerbating the matter, Monty was the mortician at work. The whole situation felt like an outbreak of plague. The last time Amy had been here was at Charlie's behest to make sure Monty was doing her job correctly and not just blowing him off, which she clearly had been. That had been the Jack of Hearts case. She'd just buried Harry and she was right back here, now with the body of a dead girl. A dead girl with Shilling's name carved in her chest. Everyone was looking at him like he'd done it.

She'd left Charlie outside. Monty still didn't want him in her morgue, and, honestly, he shouldn't be there. Not for this. She'd never seen him so rattled. His coat lay on the table next to the slab that held Esther's body.

Police evidence now. There was residue from the corpse on it, and fibres from the coat on her body. Less than ideal.

"Think you'll actually get him this time?" Monty sighed, laying down her tools and stripping off her gloves.

"What?" Amy looked up wearily.

"Freakshow," the mortician replied. "Do you think you can finally get him this time? Thanks for keeping him out of the office, by the way."

"Don't start, Monty…" Amy threatened. "I swear to God…"

"What? You can't tell me you and your dad aren't looking to get payback for what he did to Harry," Monty insisted.

Amy willed herself to take a breath. She was too tired for this. She willed herself not to pick up Monty's scalpel and stab her with it. Slowly and painstakingly, she bit out a sentence.

"What, exactly, in the evidence before you, makes you think Charlie had anything to do with this?" she hissed.

"You're looking at the same body I am, right?" Monty checked. "The little girl who was tortured to death? The one with his name carved into her chest, who was brought in wrapped in his coat?"

"She was wrapped in his coat because, when we found her, he couldn't bear to see her like that and insisted on getting her down," Amy snapped. "Officer Bond and I saw him do it. There are witnesses to —"

"To his tampering with evidence?" Monty raised an

eyebrow. "With a body that he literally carved his name into?"

"He didn't do this!" Amy yelled. "He didn't do that! This poor girl was… was left as some kind of warning note to him!"

"From one serial killer to another?" Monty probed. "Come on, Florin. This wasn't a first-time murder. No one goes from minding their own business to torturing a kid to death. Whoever did this has killed before. Gruesomely. How many serial killers do you think London is home to? You think we just breed a neighbourhood of human butcherers? Shilling just happens to have a knack for finding them? Last time I saw you, you were here helping him look into a killer. Next thing, your fiancé is pinned for it and then just happens to die before he can be brought to trial? Suddenly, there's a brand-new body and a fresh killer? Doc, look, I know you must be a mess, I know your life has been ruined, but are you really letting him manipulate you so effectively you can't see he's the one killing these people?"

Amy leant on the edge of the slab, breathing slowly and trying not to cry. Monty stepped toward her, like she was thinking about comforting her, but then seemed to reconsider and stepped away again, pretending to look busy and hide that she had cared. Amy was grateful. If Monty had tried to touch her, she felt like she would have snapped. It seemed like an eternity passed before her throat unclenched enough that she could speak again.

"You liked Harry, didn't you?" she whispered.

"I mean…" Monty half turned back to her. "I wouldn't pretend I knew him like you did. We were probably more acquaintances than friends, but…"

"But Harry was charming," Amy finished. "Harry was personable and charismatic, and Charlie is awkward and stubborn. He doesn't suffer fools, he's dismissive, and you don't like him. But you liked Harry, and I'm guessing, Monty, that you can count the number of people you actually like on your fingers." She looked up to find Monty considering this with ruefully pursed lips. "But that doesn't mean that someone's a killer just because you don't like them. Charlie… he's different, I know—"

"If you're about to do the bit where you explain how he has a singular intellect, please remember who else gets described like that," Monty warned.

"Charlie isn't a killer, Monty," Amy insisted. "He's lots of things, I will concede. He is obsessive and compulsive and difficult but… but he's fragile. He's so fragile and I know it manifests as distant and callous, but I promise you that's just most people's inability to read him. It's quite the opposite. Charlie doesn't hurt people. He wants to fix things. That's why he does the things he does. This… this broke him, Monty."

Monty shook her head. "Doc…" she sighed wearily.

"Come and see him, and tell me you think he did this," Amy insisted.

Monty was already scoffing at her, but Amy strode straight for the door and didn't look back. She felt the mortician follow her as she headed up the corridor. The building was locked up for the night and no one else was around. It was as dark and creepy as any morgue in the middle of the night, but Amy was too... too something to be scared. Too angry maybe? Too overwhelmed with the battling powers of grief raging through her to feel anything like fear in the face of things as small as mortality or superstition.

She led Monty into the lobby. Faint orange light from the streetlamps outside filtered through the windows. It was the only light in the otherwise dark room. Charlie was slumped on a hard wooden bench against the wall. He had his face in his hands and his elbows on his knees. His usually messy hair was approaching startled scarecrow in appearance, as though he'd been resting his fingers in it. He looked up when they entered. His sleeves were wet and his eyes were red and raw, like he'd been sitting on the bench crying on and off for hours. His skin looked blotchy and sickly, washed out in his funeral clothes, and he was shivering without his coat. Although, it could be from the shock as much as the cold. He registered them with dead eyes, and sunk back into himself.

"Charlie..." Amy whispered, crossing to his side instantly. He shied away from her, curling into his knees.

"Don't touch me..." he muttered.

She ignored his protests and pulled him close, sliding her arms around his shoulders. God, he was freezing, and he rattled like his bones were powered by clockwork. The protests were all verbal. They eased as she pulled him in, and he didn't fight her. She wanted to say something to comfort him, to try and make it better, but it felt awfully futile.

"We…" she whispered, pausing to clear her throat. "The autopsy… we… a lot of the damage was caused post-mortem." It felt like a weak attempt, but was the best she could think of.

"Don't kid yourself, doc," Monty broke the illusion. "Plenty of it wasn't. Don't pretend it was an easy way to go."

Amy glared at her with all the fury her pain could muster. She was pleased to note Monty had the sense to look ashamed, even before she glared. The mortician seemed genuinely uncomfortable. Amy could live with that. She could live with the way Monty struggled to look at Charlie, like it involved confronting something she didn't want to admit.

Charlie's breath became weak and ragged again. He wiped at his wet face with his already damp sleeves. Amy held him while he cried. She couldn't imagine what he must be feeling. He'd known Esther. He'd thought well enough of her to be polite to her at dinner parties — not a feat for which he was notorious. Amy didn't blame him for what had happened, but she felt like the only person who didn't, including him. He looked like he blamed himself, and she didn't know how to convince him otherwise.

Monty wasn't helping. However, she wasn't hindering either. She was just standing awkwardly to the side, a lot more like Charlie than she'd ever want to admit. She looked guilty and unnerved, as though watching Charlie display anything but impatience disturbed her understanding of the world.

A shadow fell across the middle of the hall. It was the only clue that the sound was coming. Charlie must have realised, but Amy jumped when the knock came at the door. It was sharp, echoing. Damning. Far too loud to be a branch against the window. A deliberate request to enter the locked morgue.

Monty pulled the keys from her pocket and unlocked the door, opening it widely and bowing slightly. Clearly, she could see the knocker through the small window above the handle. Still, Amy was surprised she recognised the silhouette that stepped through the doorway.

"Lord Pound," Monty greeted him respectfully.

"Monty, thank you for staying so late," Henry sighed. "We missed you at the service."

"Oh, uh—" Monty stuttered. "Apologies, my Lord, I uh— I wasn't sure it was really my place, what with… uh… I am sorry for your loss."

"Thank you," Henry replied with the energy of someone who had spent all day responding to that statement. He stepped further into the room, his cane tapping on the polished stone floor, and turned in the half-light to face Amy and Charlie.

"Daddy…?" Amy half rose, but she couldn't quite bring herself to let Charlie go.

Pound looked them over and his expression was a mystery. Charlie raised his head to meet Henry's eye. Something in Pound's face softened as he took in Charlie's condition.

"We got your message, Charles," he sighed. "I've talked to the Commissioner."

"Then we're going," Charlie announced, tearing himself from Amy's arms as he lurched jerkily to his feet.

"It's the middle of the night, Shilling," Henry sighed, motioning him down. "Farthing is organising a visit in the morning, but there has been no sign of suspicious activity. We'll get you in tomorrow, lad, but only on the condition that you go home and get some rest tonight."

Charlie swayed blearily on his feet. He looked set to protest, but also didn't quite seem to know what he should be protesting.

"Come along, you two," Henry coaxed.

Amy flashed back to the way he used to convince her and Harry to heed him as children. The exact same tone and manner. The same endless, quiet patience, tempered with unquestionable sternness. Even in the ominous, half-dark morgue, he was the most familiar, comforting presence. She stood to join him as though in a trance. He held out an arm and she flung herself into his embrace, catching him around the waist and burying her face against his chest.

"Amelia, darling..." he sighed at her, squeezing her gently.

She let him go and they both looked over to check Shilling, who hadn't moved. He was still swaying like a drunkard and shaking his head.

"Can't go yet," he muttered. "Have to formally identify the body. Can't let the Galliums do it."

"They're her next of kin, Shilling," Monty told him, her civil tone probably more a mark of her respect for Pound than anything else. "Once the Crown is done with their investigation, her body belongs to them."

"They can't see her like that," Charlie insisted, his voice tinged with exhausted hysteria. "They can't. You can't let them see that. You can't ask them to. Let me identify her."

"She's already identified, Fre—" Monty cut herself off with a nervous glance at Florin and Pound. "She's already been identified, Mister Shilling." The mortician paused awkwardly for a moment, letting the discomfort hang in the air for all of them to feel. "But… but I guess I take your point. Esther Gallium stays with me for now anyway. I can't keep them from seeing her forever though."

"I don't need forever," Charlie growled. "I just need a day or two until I work out how she did it."

"How who did what?" Amy asked. "Charlie… Esther died of obvious causes—"

"Esther was killed by Lubov Kopeck," Charlie spat the name like a curse. "I know she did it, I just need to work out how."

Amy looked up at her father. Henry's expression was grim and there were traces of concerned doubt lingering at the corners of his eyes and mouth. She was about to ask when she saw Monty's face. The mortician had barely been able to summon sympathy for Charlie when she'd seen him weeping, but at his statement the blood had drained from her face. All contempt had vanished and replaced itself with sick fear. Even if she didn't like Charlie, it almost looked like she might believe him.

6

Shilling didn't think he would be able to sleep at all. When the morning came, he wished he hadn't. He woke with sandy eyes and a throbbing headache, his heart racing from endless nightmares, and tear stains across his pillow. Rebecca was in his room, sitting on the side of his bed and rubbing his back like he'd been crying in his sleep. His mouth tasted awful, dry and bitter. He'd bathed before bed, but he swore he could still smell the sewers. Particles trapped in his nasal passages, no doubt. Traces of the underground and Esther and the morgue.

He buried his face in his pillow, breathing in the soothing perfume he sprinkled it with. Florin's perfume. The warm floral scent of lavender, rose, and chamomile. In the darkness, shambling corpses still chased him through endless tunnels. Underground caverns collapsed in on him, burying him alive. Decomposing bodies tumbled through the holes in piles, falling mutilated, white-eyed, and slack-jawed around him. Over him. He could feel himself shivering wildly under Becky's comforting touch. Nightmares and memories fought in his mind for dominance, each one hoping to outdo the other in gruesomeness. He whimpered into the pillow.

"Sue's with Abraham and Constance," Becky whispered. "She'll help look after them. Things are going to be okay, Charlie."

"Why do people always say that when someone dies?" Charlie muttered.

"Because it's true," she replied, her hand making small circles over his spine. "And you know it. I don't envy you the messes you've lived through, Charlie. I don't envy you your yesterday. Losing people hurts. If even half of what they said about Esther was true—"

"It's worse," Charlie interrupted abruptly. "It's worse than they're saying." He rubbed his face on the pillow once more, erasing the last of his tears, before shuffling up and clambering from the bed. "I have to go. I have to get ready."

"You're going to do something brave and stupid, aren't you?" Becky disapproved.

"I'm going to do anything I can to rectify this," Charlie muttered. "I can't save Esther, but I can get her killer. If there is even a shred of justice to be had, I will deliver it as best I can."

It took him a moment of struggling between nightclothes and day clothes to realise Rebecca was watching him with an unusual severity. He was slow and tired today — distracted. He couldn't afford to be distracted today. Not going up against Kopeck. But Kopeck was the distraction. His brain was on her and he couldn't shift it. He looked up, partway through buttoning his waistcoat, and regarded Becky. She was regarding him.

"That's... very old testament of you, Charlie," she said with a note of warning.

"How so?" he replied, finishing his buttons.

"Father always warned us that an eye for an eye made everyone blind," Becky reminded. "Vengeance belongs to God. It is her purview."

"Then she should do something about it," Charlie replied, grabbing his battered pale coat and swinging it on. "Due to a disturbing lack of evidence that she exists, or that Father was right, I'm going to make do with what is in my power."

"You're going to let the justice system take action?" she suggested hopefully.

Charlie glared at her.

"I thought so," Rebecca sighed. "Charlie, I can't let you go if I know you're going to break laws."

"I didn't say I would," he retorted. "I said I would get justice for Esther. For Esther, Becky. Because someone tortured a little girl to death just to get to me!"

"Because they want you stupid, Charlie," Rebecca sighed. "Because she wants to beat you. She did something she knew would get under your skin. She did something she knew would rattle you until you were prepared to do something stupid. Are you going to do something stupid, Charlie?"

He paused while he processed that. Unfortunately, Rebecca was right. He hated that she could do that. His fingers stroked his coat buttons, nearly every finger on a button. Fingers sharing buttons, moving like he was playing a flute or working clay. The tips of his fingers scratched at the smooth surface, stimming the polish like it was glass that could numb the nerves there. He stayed there, circling, circling, circling… circling.

Rebecca was still watching him.

"I can't just…" he breathed, tears hovering in his voice again. "I don't—"

There was a knock from downstairs.

His fingers stopped. The siblings shared a look and moved from the bedroom. The landing outside Charlie's room had a good view down the stairs straight to the front door. They saw Jasper open the door. Charlie was already moving down the stairs. He couldn't stop himself. Something in his gut told him that whatever lay on the other side of the door was important. The most important thing there was. Jasper pulled the door wide.

"Good morning, Doctor," he greeted her politely.

"Florin!" Charlie burst through the doorway, catching her around the waist before he realised what he was doing.

"Charlie?!" She startled as he embraced her. Her surprise should have been a warning to him, but he was already clinging to her, his face already pressed to her cheek, lost in the dark auburn curls pinned carefully around her head. She smelled like his pillow, but better, and she was warm and comforting, despite the boning of her corset stabbing him in the ribs. Her arms settled delicately around his shoulders, but the longer they stood there the more her posture softened and her grip tightened. "Oh, Charlie…" she sighed. "Are you all right?"

The profound concern in her voice snapped him

back to reality and he let her go. Everyone was staring at him. Even Jasper looked gobsmacked. There wasn't a single snide remark hanging about him, and his eyes were creased with worry.

"Sorry…" Charlie muttered, stepping back and clutching a button as he dropped his eyes. "That was inappropriate."

"No, Charlie, it's fine," she assured him. Her hand rested against his arm, squeezing his shoulder gently. "Truly, it's fine. Are you okay?"

Oh God, she was doing her doctor voice. She knew he wasn't all right, but she wasn't about to diagnose his trauma in the doorway. She was trying to get him to ask for help, to say that he needed something, but all he needed was to rewind time and save Esther and he didn't know how to ask for that, or how to ask for the therapy that could make him not need that anymore, but honestly he wasn't sure it would be right not to need that.

"It's good to see you, Florin," Charlie muttered, unable to make eye contact and urgently rubbing his coat button. "But I'm afraid I have to head off. I—"

"I have letters from Daddy and Commissioner Farthing," Florin interrupted him. "And a carriage to take us out to Goldmark Prison. Augusta has just popped into the bakery for travel snacks." She gestured behind her to the Pound family carriage parked outside the Pence bakery across the road. "Is there something else you need?"

Charlie stared at her. He couldn't stop staring. God, he could kiss her right now. He wanted to. He couldn't imagine a single more incredible person had ever existed. She just *knew* everything. She was always on the same step as him. No one else had ever kept up with such ease. She was brilliant, so brilliant, impossibly brilliant, and she was beautiful. Her red curls and her black freckles and her fierce eyes were so charming. So alluring. The questioning pout of her lips was entrancing.

Except the inappropriateness of his behaviour had already been scandalous, and throwing himself at her in such a manner would be unseemly on a level he could not bring himself to entertain. The last thing he needed in his current storm of anguished madness was to drive off the wisest collaborator he'd ever had. Instead, he just stared at her. He stared at her so long he could feel other people growing uncomfortable.

He was staring at Florin, and Jasper was staring at him, and Florin... Florin's eyes moved from his, breaking her inquisition of him, and looked past him. He broke his contemplation of her to follow her gaze.

Rebecca stood at the bottom of the stairs, holding her robe carefully closed over her nightdress. She shared a look with Florin. A severe and concerned look that seemed to speak volumes in a language Shilling wasn't fluent in. Florin nodded once, like she understood. Of course she did. Of course she spoke Rebecca. The women were talking with their eyes like they were psychically linked. Becky used to do that with her colleagues at the High House too. He had been assured they weren't telepathic and dismissed the theory as unlikely. However, the evidence was suspicious.

Florin looked back at him, and there was something in her eyes he couldn't read. She was trying to communicate with him the same way, he just didn't know how it worked. He couldn't quite link the minute muscle movements to specific articulations — beyond the understanding that both women were worried about him.

"What is it, Florin?" he asked.

She didn't speak, but her expression softened, settling into something patient and accepting. Her lips stretched, more a grimace than a smile, but it felt like she was trying. Then she touched his cheek. One gloved hand rested softly against the side of his face as she looked at him. Her action triggered a physical reaction in him. Although he wasn't sure there were any outward tells, it felt like his bones slowly melted to syrup from the point of contact down. His knees went weak and he wasn't sure he could move, but if he didn't he might collapse.

"Oh Charlie..." she sighed.

And just like that her hand left his face. The absence of her touch was abruptly cold and confusing and he missed it instantly. Instead, she slipped her hand into his, squeezing his fingers reassuringly and leading him from the house. Overall, it was an incredibly confusing interaction, but his legs were too weak to refuse, and she seemed to be dragging him exactly where he had intended to go anyway.

Rebecca and Jasper said nothing and made no attempt to stop them. Jasper still looked like he'd been slapped with a fish, and, honestly, stunned surprise was a nice change from the usual contempt. Perhaps he was behaving in front of Rebecca, or perhaps he had heard about Esther and was showing uncharacteristic compassion.

Charlie let Florin drag him across the road and into the carriage. They settled in the back seat and a woman Shilling recognised as Pound's chauffeur, who must have been Augusta, handed him a paper bag of warm butter knots through the window. Charlie sat in the back of the carriage with Florin, holding the bag, gently smelling the bag, and felt like perhaps he needed to start crying again as the carriage began slowly rolling off down the road.

His fingers trembled as he unrolled the curled top of the brown paper parcel and pulled it open. A warm cloud of buttery steam met his nose. He held out the open bag to Florin, who politely yet insanely declined with a shake of the head and gesture of a glove. He wasn't going to question it. If it hadn't been bread, he probably wouldn't have felt like eating either. But it was bread. Fresh Pence bread.

He took out a knot and bit into it. It didn't make him cry, but he did whimper slightly. It was crusty and fluffy and savoury and good, and he was alive and Kopeck and the sewers and the underground hadn't killed him. But they had killed Esther. The memory of her gave the bread a bitter aftertaste. He wondered how long that would last. If, perhaps, everything would have a bitter aftertaste for a while. At least until he got Kopeck.

"Charlie…?" Florin inquired gently beside him.

He glanced to her, framed perfectly by the drapes of the carriage window, the light from outside catching her hair and silhouetting her like an angel. He couldn't spare her more than a glance this time. Couldn't stare like before. No. Not now. If he did that now, he'd go mad again. Hysterical, probably. Instead, he kept his attention on the bread, holding it close to his face, shredding it in his fingers and wolfing it down like he hadn't eaten in days.

Florin sighed patiently at his side, turning her face so that she could watch the city pass by out the window.

"Daddy told me about Kopeck," she admitted. "Before he gave me the letters, he explained. She… she was your first case with the police. The missing kids… I remember reading about it in the paper. No one else realised they were all connected…"

"No one else cared," Charlie muttered around his bread. "It had been going on for years. Lubov Kopeck had been trafficking children into slavery for years. But they were poor kids. Orphans, kids from poverty-stricken areas, kids she could convince the world no one would miss." He very suddenly didn't feel like bread anymore. It was sitting heavy and lumpy in his stomach.

"You cared, Charlie," Florin insisted. "You cared, and you stopped her. You found the trafficking tunnels and —" She stopped abruptly.

He knew what she'd been about to say. He'd found Kopeck's tunnels. Found where she'd been hiding the kids. Then she'd collapsed the tunnels on them. He hadn't liked going underground even before that. It had been worse since. He'd had to make decisions that day. He'd had to choose between helping dying children or pursuing Kopeck. Statistically, more lives were saved by incarcerating Kopeck and stopping her operation.

Tell that to Esther.

Tell that to the children that hadn't left those tunnels. Some had made it. Charlie had made it. Sometimes it didn't feel like it. Every time he had to go back underground… it felt like he hadn't made it.

"She's still in prison, Charlie," Florin told him carefully. "Daddy and Farthing both made calls. They checked. We're going to see her. You have visitor access to discuss it with her, but she couldn't have done this. Not by herself."

"No one else would have left me the body of a child as a letter, Florin," Shilling murmured, his mouth dry and bitter again. "There has to be something."

"Well… there is… something," Florin admitted.

Charlie turned to stare at her. The tone of her voice overrode all angelic distraction. She pulled a face at his expression. Her reluctance was plain, because she made no attempt to hide it, and he was certain it was just because she was still worried about him.

"Kopeck was moved to death row two weeks ago," she confessed. "She's to be hanged in three days. No chance of appeal."

Something settled in Charlie and he shoved the entire rest of the knot into his mouth, cheeks bulging as he chewed slowly. He remembered Kopeck's case. He had watched all her appeals fail. He knew she'd been sentenced to hang. It was one of the few times he hadn't had any complaints about capital punishment. All attempts at reformation had been as pointless as her appeals. She was, as fully as he could fathom, a genuine monster.

Just like Harry Pound.

Not that he was going to say that to Florin. But the two of them had vanquished that monster, and fate had put the fiend in the ground. If Kopeck had managed to get a message to an acquaintance while she was being moved, they could find and vanquish that monster too. Then, in three days, fate could put another fiend in the ground.

7

Goldmark Prison was, well... a prison. Amy hadn't been to a prison before, and she wasn't enthused about the idea. It was unsettling in the extreme, but the thought of letting Charlie try and do any of this alone was impossible. Rebecca had asked her to look after him, practically begged her. Perhaps not in words, but the meaning had been plain. She couldn't back out now, not when he was such a mess.

Besides, in reality, Goldmark wasn't nearly as bad as she had imagined. The compound's exterior was grim, certainly, but inside was painted better than several churches she'd seen. The routine inside also involved a lot of showing the letters to various people, and then sitting and waiting while those people got their superiors; which was surprisingly relaxing.

They were in their third waiting room. Every space they had been in so far was covered with religious iconography and art. It was unexpectedly inspirational. She couldn't help but comment on it.

"Hm," Charlie mused in reply, slouching in his seat and twisting his ring. "It's part of the rehabilitation program," he muttered. "They get artists to design murals and take classes of inmates — teaching them to paint before allowing the best to contribute to the wall art."

"Some of these are incredible…" Amy marvelled, still gazing around the room.

"Notice a theme?" Charlie sulked.

"They're all religious paintings," she noted. "I know the Church help run most of England's prisons though."

"Repent or burn," Charlie muttered, calling attention to the many and varied depictions of Hell represented throughout the building.

Amy pursed her lips as she considered that. It probably wasn't an awful idea to find an artful way to encourage rehabilitation. Although, she did wonder if staring down the pictograph of choice between Atonement or Hellfire did start to desensitise some people.

"You know another recurring theme I notice…" she mused. "Prevalent here as well as so much of the world…"

"Hm?" Charlie turned to her curiously.

Amy eyed a spread across one wall, watching the fall of Lucifer on one side and the rise of the same figure with horns and a tail on the other — their wings burnt from lustrous and feathery white to black and batlike.

"Have you noticed that Satan in every iteration and gender is always naked and attractive?" she pondered, contemplating aspects of Hell they could possibly have worked a little harder to make less appealing. "What does that tell you?"

"A lot about artists," Charlie replied.

The door opened and Charlie was on his feet before Amy could laugh at his quip. She followed suit, and they were met by a tall man in neutral grey attire and two guards.

"Apologies," he greeted them. "I did know you were coming. Today just seems to have gotten away from me a little bit."

"Warden," Charlie greeted him with the enthusiasm of a dead goat. "Did you inadvertently discover the correlation between poverty and crime?"

"Charles," the Warden responded in kind. "Always a pleasure." It wasn't. Half of Spain could probably tell that from here. He ignored Charlie's jab. The displeasure melted away from the tall man's face as he turned to Amy. "Doctor Florin, it's an honour." He kissed her hand when she held it out to meet him. "I heard about the funeral. Sorry for your loss."

"Thank you," Amy sighed, wishing that was further behind them than it was.

"Lord Pound said it was essential that you speak to Lubov Kopeck," the Warden frowned apprehensively. "I'm afraid you'll have to come through to maximum security. I'm having her brought to interrogation through there, but I cannot bring her out to you."

"Obviously," Charlie rolled his eyes.

Amy just nodded, grateful for her sake that the Warden was happy to walk her through basic protocol, even if it was aggravating Charlie. He was easily aggravated, presently. She didn't blame him. After everything she'd heard about Kopeck and Charlie, she wasn't surprised he was a mess. After what she'd seen last night, she was surprised it wasn't worse. The sight of Esther in the tunnel was going to haunt her for a long time. She'd come to that realisation seeing the girl laid out at the morgue. For Charlie, it wasn't a single horror. It was a rekindling of an old and terrible horror. Something bone deep. Something that stacked through his soul, so much bigger than him.

They were escorted by the Warden and his guards further into the prison. The jiggling of keys and rattle of bars began to echo in the back of Amy's mind as they travelled. It was foolish, mad even, but the sense of entrapment grew. It was pervasive. In the air. She knew she wasn't staying. She knew it was a short visit. But here, down in these parts, sunlight felt a long way away, and the murals of hellfire did nothing to warm the cold concrete walls.

At her side, she could feel Charlie shrinking. Not in size, but in energy. She knew he was staunchly anti-prisons. That was one of the first things she'd learnt about him, all those years ago, when her father had initially tested the working relationship of Shilling and the Police. He was an excellent detective. Unparalleled. But he wouldn't join the force. He wouldn't behave. Ever the raging anarchist, he would engage in screaming matches with her father and Harry over the oppression of imperialism.

She remembered one such argument a couple of years ago. Henry had wanted Charlie's help to catch someone, and Shilling had refused. They'd been fighting about it down in his office while Amy had been trying to study for her exams. In her memories, she could still hear Charlie's voice ringing through the halls. He'd told Henry that he needed to disestablish the monarchy and redistribute the Crown's wealth to combat crime. The system was busy taking better care of its incarcerated than its citizens. In prison, everyone was entitled to a bed and three meals a day. Inmates were rehabilitated and given an education. They were taught to cook and clean, to read and write, basic numeracy, art — the poor were practically encouraged to a life of crime because it was the fastest and easiest way to better themselves, and the system was set up to funnel them through this path in an effort to keep them oppressed.

No wonder the Warden hated him.

No wonder Charlie hated the Warden. His pain had been worn plain across him since before she'd picked him up this morning, but now it was bubbling into anger. She could see him shrinking into the simmering pot of rage. He wore it on his face. In his eyes. His eyes were anguished. She wondered if the dilemma plagued him.

While she could privately admit the validity of his arguments regarding poverty-induced crime, the obvious question in this situation still remained: what about people like Kopeck? A different conversation, she could agree, even if she was just conversing with him in her imagination. Completely different issues. However, the question remained, and it felt painfully relevant.

They were led into a chamber that was cut in half by a wall of steel bars. On each side, a table was bolted to the floor, both facing each other to promote the illusion of shared space. It very clearly was not. The division was undeniable. There wasn't even a locked gate by which people could pass from one side of the room to the other. No one was getting through without sawing through the bars. Amy felt like it should have made her feel safer, but somehow it was even more disturbing.

She and Charlie sat themselves at the table in their half of the room. The Warden and the guards waited patiently behind them. The atmosphere had the quality of nails on a chalkboard. She felt like her skeleton was flinching. Mostly from dread. She didn't know what to expect, either from Kopeck or Charlie, or even the prison staff.

Her eyes drifted to the mural along the side wall. A giant, life-sized demon with a whip thrashed and stepped on masses of cowering prisoners who crawled helplessly through a flaming wasteland that could have been Dante's sixth circle. It should have been horrifying, but it wasn't. Once again, the demon was naked and alluring — a voluptuous woman with horns and a forked tail, her full chest boldly pronounced in a way that tickled Amy's well-established bi-curiosity. Surely, somewhere, the mural designers were having a laugh. They had to be.

It added to the surreal quality of the experience. The visit was starting to feel like a nightmare that should have been frightening but was morphing into the perverse. It only got worse when the door on the other side opened. Two guards escorted a large blonde woman in chains to the table on the other side of the bars. They sat her down and fixed her shackles to the bolted table.

Charlie was standing the instant she entered the room. He moved so fast his chair banged. Too fast for Amy to try and calm him. The instant she saw his face, she didn't want to. He didn't speak until the guards stepped back, but she knew what he was going to say before he said it. She could see it in his expression.

"Who are you?" Charlie demanded.

"I am Lubov Kopeck," the woman smirked at him with a bad Russian accent.

"You're not Kopeck," Charlie shook his head. "What is this?" he demanded of the room.

"This *is* Kopeck, Shilling," the Warden assured, stepping forward. "I know it's been years since you saw her but—"

"This isn't Kopeck," Charlie insisted.

"Hello, Shilling…" the woman teased him across the table. "Did you get my note?"

Amy leapt up and caught Charlie around the chest before he threw himself at the bars. All the guards had lurched towards them, but Amy had him. Charlie wasn't a big man. He was strong and wiry, but she was perfectly capable of wrangling him. He didn't pull too hard at her grasp anyway. She kept her arms around his ribs, holding him tightly to her. He didn't try to untangle himself, seemingly understanding that she was stopping him from doing something unbelievably stupid. She could feel his chest heaving and his heart racing as she held him, and he glared daggers through the bars. The woman on the other side was laughing at him.

"Oh Shilling…" the woman purred. "You don't look so good. Something bothering you?"

This time Charlie ignored her, or at least didn't let her bait him into anything. He was slowly getting his breath back as he stepped away from Amy. She let him go cautiously, reluctant to take her hands from him as she watched him. His brain was churning. His face moved only to breathe as emotions chased each other through his mind faster than he could process. When he looked up, his eyes found the Warden.

"Kopeck ran her appeals from Steelgate before she was transferred to you," Charlie announced. It wasn't a question. "If this is the woman you received, then that means the real Kopeck has been out of custody for at least two weeks — probably using the transfer to escape and switch out."

"Wha—?" The Warden stared, gobsmacked.

"Oh, Shilling…" the woman called sadly through the bars. "You're not happy to see me? I'm happy to see you!"

Charlie ignored her, keeping his attention on the Warden.

"Call Pound, call Farthing, tell them everything," Charlie ordered. "Tell them there's been a breakout. Kopeck doesn't just have an accomplice out there — she's out there. She's coming for me personally. I want officers Pound trusts with my family."

"Wha—" the Warden still stuttered.

"Herman!" Charlie slapped the back of his own hand in front of the man's face to jerk him from his stupor. "Are you listening?! Right now! Get a message to

Commissioner Farthing and Lord Pound *this instant*! Kopeck has escaped and people are in danger!"

"Such a fuss, Mister Shilling," the prisoner taunted. "You'd think someone did something to upset you…"

Shilling turned and walked slowly to the bars. Amy didn't stop him this time. No one did. She could see the change in him. This was the man who had caught Kopeck the first time. This was the man the papers wrote all their stories about. The woman chained to the table seemed to realise this as well. Her smirk slipped as he approached the bars, sizing up that this scrawny young man in his battered tan coat with his messy straw hair was somehow… dangerous. It was his eyes. They'd gone stormy. The woman flinched when he looked at her.

"The first time I caught Kopeck, I brought down her operation knowing a few of her cronies escaped." He spoke with cool detachment, as though he had abruptly spent his emotional allowance for the day. "I don't know how she bought or blackmailed you into taking her place. That only interests me with regard to the methods used to execute this plan." He lifted his chin. The prisoner definitely wasn't smiling anymore. "Someone has already died because of what you helped Kopeck do, and you will answer for that. Then, in three days, if I have not found the real Lubov Kopeck, you will hang for her too. Let me know if I should leave her in her tunnels for the week before bringing her back into custody."

8

The Bakery felt like the safest place to be, but Shilling wasn't sure he wanted to feel safe right now. Feeling safe felt wrong. Pound had agreed to station officers at Shilling's house to look out for his sisters, but given that Esther had been the first victim, it was hard to know who needed protecting from the escaped killer. Charlie was presently trying to convince Julian and Michael to take extra care given the circumstances.

"I promise you, Sleuth, we don't need to be scared of the mean old Russian lady," Julian assured, lounging on the bed while Skipp sorted through notes on the desk.

Charlie frowned at them, but Julian just pulled a face back, and Michael wasn't looking. He was slumped behind the desk, combing through his notes, and pulling his own faces.

"There's nothing," he muttered. "I have nothing on her. Not from anyone. No street gossip. No one has no street gossip about them."

"Unless they're making sure nothing gets out," Shilling replied. "Kopeck might be paying people to keep quiet, or there might be a stack of bodies we haven't found yet."

"Everything we do have suggests she's not above

killing for convenience," Michael agreed.

"She's not," Charlie grimaced. "She'd kill out of boredom. She will definitely kill for pleasure or entertainment. She killed Esther for fun — because she enjoys torturing. She would do it again — she will try and do it again — and she believes in escalation. Swift, I cannot impress upon you enough how dangerous this woman is."

"Well, you've got officers outside your house, and our good doctor returned home — I imagine daddy Pound has uniforms protecting her too?" Julian drawled.

"I believe so," Shilling sighed, sinking down onto the edge of the bed beside Julian. "He's not a fool and he won't risk Florin's safety, thank God. I wish she'd take more care to keep out of danger herself. I know she's wise enough, but the inclination seems to be lacking."

Julian and Michael shared the wriest look in recorded history.

"God, I wonder what it's like to have a friend like that..." Julian drawled, dripping sarcasm and outstaring Michael, who dropped his eyes to hide his chuckle.

"Indeed," Mike added, shooting Charlie a look. "Pursuing the truth always comes at a price, but it would be nice to know the two of you remember to keep your wallets handy."

"I sent her home, she'll be fine," Shilling muttered, leaning on his knees and ruffling his hair.

"You sent her home?" Julian echoed incredulously, tilting towards him so that Charlie could see his raised eyebrows. "You're lucky she didn't kick you in the grapes, Sleuth. That is not a lady who likes to be ordered around."

"Better to be sent home than carved up," Shilling muttered bleakly, looking over his shoulder at Julian and adjusting himself on the edge of the bed. "Sticking around me right now isn't safe. She came to Goldmark with me this morning and that's more than enough adventure, I'm sure. I don't think she enjoyed visiting prison."

"I don't know..." Julian lounged. "I've been to Goldmark — it's not a bad prison."

Charlie and Michael both shot him surprised looks.

"All prisons are bad," Charlie said automatically.

Julian rolled his eyes at their expressions. His face could be truly scathing when it wanted to be, but at least he was kind enough to temper it with love.

"Not like that." He pouted in response to their astonishment. "I've visited as an art student. Some of the murals in that place are truly..." he trailed off longingly.

"Yes, they do look rather like something you would commission for your bedroom ceiling," Charlie commented drily. "Florin may have made a passing comment of that ilk while we were there."

"Told you she's a proper lass," Julian grinned. "Bet she wouldn't mind letting you paint her bedroom ceiling..."

"What is that even supposed to mean?" Charlie turned to him in exasperation.

He was met with a pout of tragic disappointment

from Julian, who clearly thought he'd been quite obvious, and who replied by reaching out with one large, spread hand, gently grabbing Charlie's face, and pushing him over onto the bed in dismissal. Charlie protested, but it came out as a muffled whine as he was tenderly manhandled.

"Julian's being rude," Mike clarified unnecessarily from the desk. "But he's not wrong. You and Doctor Florin have a lot in common."

"Not quite what I meant, love," Julian sighed. "I was suggesting they could have a bit more in common — if you know what I mean."

"You were alluding to the fact that they fancy each other," Michael smiled. "Yes, dear, we know."

"We do not!" Charlie huffed, untangling himself from Julian and trying to straighten his hair.

Michael laughed, really laughed, and Julian groaned with such violent cynicism that Charlie spooked beside him. Michael laughed harder. Charlie opened his mouth to protest further, but Julian flicked him in the ear and his words morphed into a pained exclamation.

"Yes, you do, Charles," Michael told him. "I've known you far too long for you to try and pretend to me now that you don't fancy her."

Charlie flushed angrily, holding a protective hand over his ear. He glared at his friends, but Julian was smirking at him and Michael was all but ignoring him, still focused on his piles of information.

"Florin is a dear friend and I admire her greatly," Charlie huffed, trying extremely hard, and completely failing, not to think about the way he had thrown himself at her this morning… and how badly he had wanted to kiss her in the doorway… and wanted to kiss her back in France… and the time that he actually had kissed her at her graduation party and then nearly run into a door during the ensuing stupor.

Julian and Michael were both looking at him now, and their expressions suggested they weren't buying it for an instant. Charlie could feel his cheeks growing hotter.

"Look, Florin is wonderful, truly, I won't argue about it!" he snapped. "But can we please all agree there are much more pressing things eventuating currently?!"

"If you're pressing things, Sleuth, I think she wants to be one of them," Julian smirked.

Charlie nearly hit him. He was sorely tempted. It had never worked before though.

"Charlie," Mike called to him warningly, breaking the tension and redirecting his attention. "You do care for her, so make sure Lord Pound's got eyes on her," he advised. "She's like you, and we know you, you're about to go bounding off into trouble to find Kopeck."

Charlie nodded slowly. That, at least, was worth considering. Except, he didn't know what he was doing, and he groaned as reality oozed over him once more.

"I don't know where to start," Shilling muttered, slouching on the side of the bed with his head in his hands, scrunching his hair. "The police are following most of the leads. An escaped prisoner is their purview. Pound said they think they know which guard Kopeck blackmailed to help her make the swap, but they've got no useful information save their own indicative terror.

She got out, went underground — literally — and there's not so much as a breath of her save the murder of Esther. I can't even work out how she knew that I knew Esther, we... we weren't exactly close."

"I'll keep digging, Sleuth," Mike assured. "I promise, we'll find something."

"Just don't put yourself or your runners in danger doing it," Charlie ordered. "I'm serious, please, Skipp. I can't have the next body we find be one of your little runners..."

Julian and Michael shared another look, and this one was finally appropriately severe.

"What are you going to do, Charlie?" Julian asked.

"I don't know," Charlie muttered, shaking his head. "I need to think. I'm going to think."

"You need any company? Sounding board? Fresh clay?" Julian offered.

Charlie shook his head again. "I think better on my own, Swift. I want you here with Skipp. You two need to look after each other — and everyone else here. Please."

"We will," Michael nodded. "Who's looking after you, Sleuth?"

"I'll be in the workshop," Charlie sighed, getting to his feet and heading for the door. "There are officers stationed right outside the house — and I imagine they will be checking in regularly. As soon as Farthing's people find something, I expect them to contact me. They might be running the investigation, but Kopeck must be the most wanted person in Britain right now. There's no way the Crown will risk leaving me in the cold if it means we could find her sooner."

Besides, Shilling added privately in his head as he farewelled his friends, I make excellent bait. He knew saying that aloud would just trouble them, but it didn't make it less true. Kopeck was after him, not just to hang him from a hook in the sewers and gut him — she would want to teach him a lesson. Esther was just the start of that. That was what revenge by Kopeck's hand looked like. She wanted him to suffer, and if it would help catch her, Commissioner Farthing would absolutely set a trap using Charlie as the tempting crumb of cheese.

These thoughts carried him back across the road and into the studio at the back of the house. Jasper hadn't set any traps recently. Not since the death of Harry Pound. The absence of antagonism was starting to make Charlie nervous. Maybe he was saving up for something really big. Maybe he had finally gotten over himself and matured past childish hostility. Maybe the truth lay in the middle, and the last few days had earned Charlie a small reprieve.

He stripped down and changed into the loose, drawstring trousers he wore for his pottery, slipping the ring from his finger and stashing it safely in his pocket. Getting clay on his regular clothes wasn't worth the hassle of his sisters and the maids. He didn't need to be cleaned up after, he needed to be left alone to clean up after himself. And they needed to stop moving his things! As he went through the motions, getting started, he wasn't sure if his frustration on the matter was characteristic or exacerbated.

Sitting at the wheel and beginning to knead the clay was instantly soothing. It was cold and wet on his hands. It squeezed between his fingers. It made him feel strangely human, like he belonged to the world still. This strange world he so often felt he didn't belong in, that he sought so desperately to understand. This fascinating and cruel reality. The world that had killed Esther Gallium.

Shilling never talked about the Kopeck case. It had gone in the small and private lockbox in the back of his mind where things he wouldn't discuss went. Rebecca and Michael had both attempted to pry before, but Charlie hadn't known how to talk about it. He didn't even know how to talk about it with Florin. She'd asked in the carriage, supplied half the conversation herself, but he hadn't been able to fill the gaps.

She'd seen his panic attack last night. Bullion and his friends had called Charlie a hysterical freak, and Florin had told him not to let anyone talk to him like that, right before he'd flown to pieces and disturbed a crime scene. Everything became tighter in the tunnels. He knew how far the walls were. Logically, he knew. He could measure them. He could calculate length and width… until they started to shrink. The longer he looked at them the tighter they became, like they were pressing down, collapsing around him. He could feel the weight of everything above him, the entire city — streets and buildings and people and earth — all hanging over him waiting to drop and crush him like slapping a spoon into jam.

He squeezed the clay in his hands, letting it squish

through his fingers, and then moulding it back together until the kaolin and water mixed evenly enough to throw. He could hear his own breathing. It was not steady. But he could fix that. He did fix it. He could hear himself settle as he began to work the wheel, shaping the clay. It covered his hands, speckling across his arms and chest. Every now and again he would try and push his hair from his eyes with the back of his wrist. He could feel faint traces of white clay smear cold and wet across his face.

None of it required thought. His brain lingered on Kopeck and Esther and Florin, dancing between terror and anger and grief and admiration… and not always in the combinations he expected. Trying to think like Kopeck, to work out where she would have gone, what she wanted, and what she was prepared to do to get it… he could respect the effectiveness, even if the ethics repulsed him. She was ruthless. On occasion, so was he. He understood that. He understood making decisions based on logical results.

Kopeck would be hiding underground. She would have returned to her old tunnels, not all of which Shilling knew and not all of which the city had mapped. She would have concocted a list of people she could use to hurt him. But why not him? Why not use the opportunity of the first attack, when no one knew she was gone, to go after him then?

Because it wouldn't hurt enough.

She wanted him to know that innocent people were dying because he'd stuck his nose in her business. The same way he could work out what she would do,

Kopeck knew he'd only caught her because he'd cared about the children she'd taken. That meant she knew that she could torture him more by making sure that he knew he was responsible for the people she was about to hurt. That's why each one had to have a personal connection to him. Kopeck had not gone to the effort of breaking out of prison and staying in London just to be subtle in her revenge.

If he was Kopeck, he would go after Florin. The thought was like a knife in his gut. She was safe. She had Lord Pound's security, and Henry would know not to risk his daughter. Not after everything else that had happened. But she was a target. Kopeck would have had access to all those stupid newspapers the last few months. If she was far enough out of the loop to believe Lionel Tanner, she probably thought Charlie and Florin were an item.

The pottery wheel stopped. So did Charlie's hands. Maybe it was because the piece was shaped and needed to be left to dry. Maybe it was because dusk was falling outside and he needed to light the room to continue into the evening. Maybe it was something else. The strange, small, and hollow heartbeat that pattered quickly like raindrops in the base of his throat. He took his clay cutter and slipped the wire under his new piece, stamping the bottom gently and setting it aside to dry.

He needed to pull the drapes and light the lamps. He did not want to pull the drapes. If he hid the windows, he would not know what might be loitering at them. But he could better light the room. Provided he even stayed here. Provided he didn't run out into the growing twilight to make sure Florin was safe. Or, at the very least, to kick Tanner somewhere very sensitive.

First things first, he had to wash the clay from his hands. He moved to the metal basin at the side of the workshop and absentmindedly scrubbed his hands, straining his ears to hear anything beyond the murky water hitting the bottom of the tub, and finding only his hollow and anxious heartbeat. The blood pounding in his ears was deafening.

The scream from upstairs was louder.

Its terror split the night.

Charlie raced barefoot up the stairs, hands still wet. He could hear screaming, struggling, and crashing. The sounds were coming from his sisters' room. Their door was open and someone was thrown into the corridor. Jasper crashed into the wall. Charlie didn't stop. He could hear his sisters screaming. He leapt Jasper and charged into the bedroom.

It was a large bedroom with a fourposter bed, a fireplace, double dressers and wardrobes. Susan was crouched behind the bed, trying to stay out of sight. Rebecca was standing in front of her, holding the poker from the fire like a weapon. A hulking woman with blonde hair was staggering back from her, clutching one arm.

"Becky!" Charlie roared, leaping unarmed to her defence.

The blonde woman turned and Charlie saw Kopeck's face leering at him. He didn't care it was a fight he couldn't win, he wasn't going to let her hurt his family. He charged her, but she threw a punch as he came rushing in. He swerved awkwardly to avoid the attack, catching her around the waist and trying to use his momentum to bring her down. It didn't work. Basic physics rallied against him. Kopeck was twice his size and raw muscle. She elbowed him sharply in the face. Pain blossomed blindingly from his nose as he fell back. He kicked out as he hit the ground, his foot connecting solidly with her ankle. She grunted but stayed standing.

Yelling sounded from downstairs. The officers from outside had been alerted. Charlie could hear them racing up to the room. Kopeck didn't go for him again. He'd expected her to try and kill him, but she was edging back. He blinked away the pain for a better view. Kopeck was holding her arm again. It was broken. That's why she hadn't attacked him properly — she couldn't.

There was an open passage partially exposed behind one of the wardrobes. A third tunnel! Charlie had never found that one. He'd never searched Susan's room. Kopeck was retreating to it. Charlie scrambled to his feet, chasing after her. Kopeck bolted, squeezing through the narrow passage and disappearing down the tight stone staircase. Charlie didn't even think. Rebecca was screaming for him, but this time the blood in his ears was louder. His bare feet raced over the cold stone stairs. It felt like flying. He barely touched them. The bitter, dusty air of the tunnel raced across his bare skin. He was halfway down before the darkness was absolute and the walls started to close in.

He froze. It was dark. So dark. There were cobwebs in his hair. There was dust from the walls mixing with the clay and water on his hands. The pressure of everything above him was compounding. He was gasping. His chest heaved. His lungs were full of the scent of earth and stone, damp and cold. It felt like being buried alive. He could feel the walls closing in, pushing against his hands. Everything was shaking. The earth trembled. He could hear rocks falling.

He was already sobbing when hands grabbed him. The instant he felt fingers snatching at him, he screamed and lurched. The hands grabbed him tighter and began to pull him, but they pulled him up. Someone was dragging him up the stairs. He could still hear himself screaming like an out of body experience. He was gasping and choking and crying, but someone had a tight hold of him and they were pulling him back into the light.

He collapsed, shivering and weeping onto the bedroom carpet.

"Charlie!" Rebecca rushed to him and fell to her knees at his side, pulling him up.

Darkness still clouded the edges of his vision and he couldn't stop hyperventilating. He was gasping fiercely, desperately, but nothing he did could get enough air into his lungs. A great weight was squeezing his bare chest and his lungs couldn't expand properly. Even with Rebecca holding him, he couldn't shift the pressure of the tunnel bearing down above him. She dug into his pocket, and a moment later she was pressing their father's old ring into his hands. His fingers began to move across the metal instinctively. It was smooth and soothing and his fingers knew the pattern and dimensions unconsciously. Rebecca helped his fingers trace the edges the way he did when he was anxious. Slowly, reality came back into focus.

The police were in the room. One officer was waiting by the passage entrance, talking softly to Susan. Two more could be heard yelling down the staircase. The person standing over him was…

"Jasper?!" he exclaimed in surprise, his voice a hoarse whisper.

The butler had a cut on his forehead that was bruising badly and trickling blood down the side of his face. He barely met Charlie's eyes. The slightest glance was cast, but instantly betrayed a powerful and genuine concern, so he looked away again.

"Glad you're unharmed, Sir," he muttered to the wall.

Charlie continued to watch him, but Jasper didn't look back. Soon enough, Susan summoned him over to inspect his injury and force him off for medical attention. Somewhere in that time, Charlie had started to breathe properly again. He wasn't sure when. Rebecca was still holding him. It felt like… like being small again. Like when they were children. Like those short few years when he had still been a child and she hadn't been anymore. When she couldn't be anymore. When father died.

Charlie curled into her, aware that he was filthy and shouldn't be getting dirt and clay on Rebecca's dress, but unable to stop himself. She pulled him in tighter, like she wasn't even aware. She was still holding him when the police came back up. Apparently the path was blocked off. There had been a trap and Kopeck had collapsed part of the tunnel behind her. Charlie felt Becky's hands squeeze him as they all realised that his panic attack might be the only reason he hadn't just been buried in rubble. That, and possibly Jasper too. The panic attack hadn't all been hallucinatory either. There really would have been falling rocks and shaking if Kopeck had collapsed part of the tunnel. But that blocked her entrance back to them as much as their access to her.

Charlie struggled to his feet. Rebecca was hesitant to let him go, and he was still shaking. His knees felt buttery and his legs were weak. There was minor staggering, consistent with traumatised stupor. Diagnosing himself felt helpful. He was still stimming the ring in one hand, but needed the other for balance. He felt dizzy.

"Charlie—" Rebecca began, following him to her feet.

"She must have been casing this place…" Charlie muttered, half to himself, but addressing his sister even as he ignored her implorations. "She knew the tunnels. She knew about this tunnel. Even I didn't know this tunnel. She got in while you were in here! She—" Charlie stopped suddenly and turned to Becky. "She was coming for you. How-how did you—?"

"I noticed the tracks on the carpet," Rebecca replied. "The wardrobe had moved an inch over, the drapes were unbound, and there were marks on the wall like something had scraped it — or it had scraped against something. I knew something was wrong, and she didn't get the drop on us like she was expecting. I hit her with the poker — multiple times, hard."

Charlie shook his head weakly. "I… I'm so glad you noticed…"

Becky gave him a wry half-smile and squeezed his shoulder.

"Of course. I'm a Shilling too, Charlie," she reminded him.

He nodded. He hadn't forgotten, he just wasn't used to her embracing that side of herself anymore. It had been years since they had both legally been Shillings. A long time had passed since her wedding. Since…

"I… I need to thank Jasper…" Charlie muttered.

"Good," Rebecca encouraged. "He's downstairs getting checked over. I want you to see a doctor too."

"Oh, no," Charlie shook his head and began to shy away from her. "No— no, I don't think—"

Rebecca grabbed him by the upper arm with her freakishly strong hands and started to manhandle him into doing her bidding worse than Julian ever did. God, Rebecca was always worse. Exactly like what he had always imagined a mother would be. Controlling. Domineering. She gave him that look too. Oh God, not the look. The look told him that not only was she going to get her way, but it was going to be worse than he'd first imagined.

9

Amy had been trying to decide between a bath or reckless disobedience when the call had come through. She had snatched her medical bag and taken two officers to accompany her straight to Lady Guinea's residence. There were significantly more officers there when she arrived, and Constable Bond met her at the door. The case was growing. Kopeck had tried to come after Charlie, or at least after his sisters. Rebecca had requested a doctor — the only doctor Charlie would talk to with any kind of cooperation.

He was filthy and startled when she saw him but, after as much of a check up as he'd let her do, she conceded that he had probably suffered a panic attack, and otherwise not much more than minor bruising — which he was nearly always home to anyway. He was edgier than normal. Jumpy and skittish, even with her. It was heartbreaking to see him that way.

"I'm fine," he told the rug resolutely as he scrunched it with his toes. His eyes stayed down. He was wrapped in a blanket and pulled it tighter about his naked torso, snuggling sulkily into it. "Can I please go wash now?"

"You can," Amy told him, setting down her small torch and surrendering her inspection of his reactions.

"Officer Tanner will accompany you while you bathe and pack a bag."

"I am not—!" Charlie began to huff.

"If Rebecca and I have to stuff you in a sack and drag you, we will," she warned him, trying to toe the line between setting him off again and using the firm hand he needed to keep him from reckless disobedience. Huh, so that's what that felt like.

Charlie glowered at her. His crooked face became even more crooked when he frowned, exacerbating the corners of his lopsided mouth and scrunching his bent nose. It was very cute. She met it with a small smile she couldn't seem to keep back at the sight of him, utterly unmoved by his plight. His grey eyes simmered, but they seemed to realise they were not going to win and he stormed off like some kind of grouchy blanket troll.

It pained her to think of what he'd been through recently, and that she hadn't been here to help him with the attack in his own home, but she couldn't say she was unhappy with how things were turning out. Guinea's residence was turning into a crime scene and Amy had convinced her father to put Charlie and his family up in their house while this case was resolved. It was easier to protect them all as a group anyway.

As tempted as she was to supervise Charlie's bath herself, it really wasn't the time or place. He was anxious enough. Although, it was Charlie, he probably wouldn't consider it bizarre or improper behaviour. The notion of why she fancied supervising might fly completely over his head. Especially if she talked to him about the case. He wouldn't even notice. Still, she knew she shouldn't be doing it, so she went to find Rebecca.

There were plenty of officers around to point her in the right direction, but she was surprised to find Shilling's sister down in his studio. The door was wide open but Amy knocked on it anyway. Rebecca was standing in the room with a few pottery tools loosely clutched in her fingers, staring at a white clay vase that was drying on a table near the window.

"Rebecca…?" Amy inquired gently as she knocked.

"Doctor Florin," Rebecca startled, breaking her trance and turning to greet her. "How is he?"

"He's Charlie," Amy shrugged. "Physically he's as well as he ever is, and everything psychological he wants to bottle up and hide from everyone."

"You just diagnosed him as English," Rebecca teased.

Amy smiled shyly. "Well, there is that."

Rebecca took the tools she was holding across to a bucket by the sink and set them away, before taking Charlie's clay cutter and carefully winding the wire around the handles to tidy it away.

"He never cleans up after himself," she murmured affectionately. "Sometimes I think he thrives in the clutter — and you've seen his room before. I'm sure, given the choice, my little Charlie would be perfectly content living as a madman." The chuckle she gave was shaky, a flimsy cover that failed to disguise her true emotions. She seemed to realise, and the look she had begun to share with Amy was quickly abandoned and downturned to hide the deep etchings of concern in her face. "You're worried about him?" she added with faux blitheness.

Amy didn't know what to say. Of course she was worried about him, but Rebecca already knew that. She wasn't really asking. She was projecting. She wanted Amy to say everything she was thinking so that she didn't feel alone in her concern. It wasn't just for Charlie. Someone had invaded her home, come after her and her wife, killed the daughter of her friends... Rebecca was doing a good job of pretending everything was about her little brother, but it wasn't. She wanted it to be though. Amy knew the feeling. She knew exactly what Rebecca was feeling after all her time dealing with Harry. They needed the attention to be on Charlie, they needed to fuss over him, because if anyone made them stop and think about what was happening, really happening, if someone asked Rebecca how she was coping... she would dissolve into tears and be unable to stop herself. Amy didn't want to do that to her. At least, not until she was safely in a new house with a bedroom door she could use to shut out invasive questions, should she so choose.

Instead, Amy approached the new vase, the object of Rebecca's contemplation before she had interrupted her.

"It's lovely," she commented, pretending to change the topic of conversation and fooling no one.

Rebecca nodded, swallowing thickly. "Yes. Quite. I had wondered if perhaps Charlie had left something unfinished when he came running, but it would seem he was done with the initial stage. It's been backstamped and set aside. I think he's trying to decide which green to add to the grooves, and whether to do it before or after firing. Possibly both."

"Which green…?" Amy commented, not quite following.

Rebecca pointed to the collection of potted paints and glazes Charlie had premixed beneath the drying table.

"Charlie does colour subconsciously," she admitted. "I don't even know if he realises he does it, but where he sits a piece to dry always seems to relate to the colours beneath the table he will eventually add. At a guess, this will be white and green." She paused a moment, a slight tightness edging into her voice. "This piece is called 'Esther'. I might see if he'll let me give it to Constance when it's done."

Amy stared at her for a moment. The piece was not named. There was nothing obvious about it to substantiate Rebecca's claims, only subtle things. Only things you could infer if you knew Charlie better than he knew himself.

"You really are a Shilling, aren't you?" Amy commented softly.

Rebecca laughed. It was a soft, choked laugh, full of tears. She was approaching breakdown point anyway, even if Amy was trying to help distract her from it.

"I'm amazed how often people forget," Rebecca smiled wryly. "Charlie forgets too. I think he thinks he's alone. I think, when I got married, he decided that it would be him against the world. I thought he was fine with it, he seemed fine with it, but after the wedding… honestly I felt like he'd gone mad overnight. He's never been the same since. The stubborn and rebellious qualities were always there, but he's just so... so wilfully lonely. I've always been grateful for the boys across the road. Now, I guess, I'm grateful for you."

"Charlie's helped me more than I've helped him," Amy replied.

"I don't think that's as true as you think," Rebecca smiled sadly, still staring at the unfinished vase.

Amy wanted to say something back, but she didn't know where to go next. She wasn't going to fight Rebecca on this, not when the woman clearly knew her brother so well. It was nice to think she was good for Charlie. She wanted to be good for Charlie. He felt good for her, even if society disagreed. It was strange how the longer anyone spent around him, the more they felt a blossoming contention with society's principles. Her angry little blanket troll.

"Does he always do this?" she gestured at the vase. "I know he throws clay to think — that it's a meditative process for him — but does he always do a piece when something big like this happens?"

"I would describe it the other way around," Rebecca replied. "All Charlie's pottery can be marked by cases and stages in his life. He's always making things, and they inadvertently reflect whatever he's working on at the time." She grimaced bleakly. "There were a lot of Jack pieces. A lot. I think Julian sold most of them — the ones Charlie didn't break, which he is prone to do. I don't think he advertised them as true to their macabre nature though, despite the number of people who might have paid highly for the perversion. Julian can be surprisingly sensitive about such things."

Amy pinched her lips together as she thought about it. It made sense. It also twisted a horrible knot in her stomach.

"He… Charlie, he gave me a vase I liked as a graduation gift… which case was that from?" she asked, needing to know but not really wanting to. She had thought the vase beautiful, and Charlie was the only thing she associated with it. She liked that about it. She loved it. But if there were dark bones hidden in its depths, she needed to know.

"The rose one?" Rebecca smiled, and the look on her face eased Amy's concern, like she could tell Amy was worried about it. "That was August two years ago. He couldn't find much work that interested him that month, so he drank a lot of cough syrup and made a lot of vases. At least half of them got smashed in frustrated tantrums since, but that one was the best and, by some miracle, he never broke it."

"That's it?" Amy blinked in surprise. "That's all there is to it?"

"That's it. You know, sometimes, he's really not as complicated as people make him out to be," Rebecca grinned.

"Who's not complicated?" Charlie's familiar and grouchy voice demanded from the doorway. "And why are you touching my stuff?! Again?!"

He strode into the room in a similar huff to when Amy had seen him leave. His hair was still wet, as though he was trying to set a new record for how fast someone could wash and change. The battered, pale coat had clearly only just gone on, and he was still attempting to get it to sit comfortably, fixing the cuffs of his shirt inside the coat sleeves.

Something about the sight of him melted her, the way it always did now. Something about his gruff pretence and scruffy exterior, and the way it completely failed to hide how soft and caring he was under it. He came striding forward, as though to scold his sister, everyone knowing full well that it wouldn't work. Amy decided to save him the trouble.

She stepped to meet him, blocking his way and catching him around the waist. She buried her face in the collar of his coat and held him exactly how she had when he had met her before Harry's funeral. This time, the scents of rain and soot and perfume were missing. Beneath the heavy aroma of soap was a faint warm smell of something that was just completely Charlie. Her embrace had clearly startled him, but she wasn't going to let that stop her. It was the same way he had grabbed her this morning. If he was allowed to surprise her like that, she was allowed to do the same to him. His arms settled around her shoulders and his damp hair pressed against her cheek. Anything he'd been about to say died on his lips, and she could feel the frustration melt out of his body. Maybe Rebecca was right. Maybe she did help him as much as he helped her.

"I don't want to go," he whispered.

"I know," she whispered back, squeezing him empathetically. "But do it for me."

He didn't say anything else, but she felt his nose tuck in closer against her jaw. She already knew he'd do it.

He hadn't wanted to go to the funeral yesterday either, he'd wanted that even less, but he'd done it anyway. He'd done it for her. Even if it went against everything in his nature to look after himself, he'd do it if she asked. Especially if she insisted.

Night had settled properly at the Pound residence. It was dark when they got there and Henry was the picture of courtesy to his guests. Charlie didn't expect anything else. Lord Pound was, after all, a gentleman. He had plenty of time and space for Lady Guinea and her wife and their staff. Plenty of time for anyone of a similar class. He had a surprising amount of time for Charlie, but Charlie didn't feel like he could return the kindness. His relationship with Henry Pound had always been comfortably antagonistic, tempered by grudging respect. They fought. They always fought, but they always got their villain in the end too.

Except last time that had been Henry's son. Little Pound Junior. Not so little after all. Charlie had caught him red handed. Harry had been sent to prison where he had, by all the evidence Charlie could uncover, taken his own life while awaiting trial. The funeral yesterday was only the second time that Charlie had heard Pound talk about his son by name since the arrest. The other time had been to tell Florin that he'd died. Henry had just... stopped. He'd stopped talking about Harry, stopped mentioning him, stopped referencing him, had all but pretended he'd never had a son. Charlie had seen the damage it had been doing to Florin, how badly it had been eating her up inside.

Now, every time Henry saw him, he had time for Charlie. Gone was the gruff, thin, and weary patience with which he used to tolerate him. Gone were the sharp rebukes and constant warnings about what Charlie could and couldn't get away with. Now, when he saw Charlie, he smiled. Now, he talked to him in a calm and soft voice that didn't quite have the stern edge that it used to.

It was all wrong. Henry should have become angrier and more hostile. He should have despised the very sight of the man who sent his son to his death. He shouldn't have gone all soft and kind and patient. Charlie didn't know what to do with that. He didn't know how to respond to it, so he was mostly avoiding it, but he was also wise enough to know that everyone could see he was avoiding it.

Strangely enough, back in the Pound's manor, his feet found their way into Harry's old office. The room he'd finally caught the Jack in. The door had been shut. And locked. And Charlie knew that should have stopped him. But it didn't. It had been stripped of a great deal of evidence post Harry's arrest, but most of the furniture was still there. It felt cold and damp and empty now. The door had probably been locked on the room since the police took the last boxes out. Months of disuse had turned the room into a memorial. Something bitter and forgotten.

He stepped slowly across the floor, looking for

anything that might settle the unease in his soul. Dark spots on the rug stopped him in his tracks. The brown marks looked black in the harsh orange light of the lamps, but he recognised his own blood. He would have died in this room if Florin hadn't burst in to save him. His plan to catch the Jack of Hearts had been deeply flawed, his mind disorientated by the length of time he'd spent on the case, mad with helplessness, stunned by the shocking revelation of the Jack's identity, and probably starting to go a bit silly over Florin already.

The sounds of Michael and Julian teasing him floated aggravatingly in the back of his brain. He pushed them away. Florin was brilliant. She made him want to be smarter, but he wasn't sure she made him wiser. If anything, it would seem to be the opposite. If he was going to catch Kopeck again, he needed to think like the man who had caught her the first time. He needed to think like the man who should have caught the Jack of Hearts.

Even as he thought it, a partial handprint in the dust on the desk made his heart flicker. He looked closer, unable to help himself, thinking of Florin in here mourning her Harry. It wasn't her handprint. Shilling blinked as he looked at it. His eyes considered the size and shape and pressure… Henry. Henry had been in there. That made more sense, and, somehow, felt worse.

Humanity seemed to have an incessant compulsion to hide their trauma. Henry was in agony, and everyone knew it, and he was pretending like nothing had happened. He was hiding the pain. That meant Florin was hiding the truth. She'd told Charlie before the funeral that she hadn't told her father about meeting her birth parents in France. She didn't want to hurt him, but the cycle would get worse. Charlie had seen it happen before. He had done it before. Except...

Well, except his case was different. It was fine. Completely fine. It didn't matter that he'd hidden his trauma from people. From the world. He had a handle on it. There weren't any dire consequences to his secrets.

He still hadn't thanked Jasper properly.

Jasper had been avoiding him.

But that was fine. Their relationship had always been difficult. They'd spent six years cultivating a bond based on Jasper's resentment and deliberate antagonism, and Charlie's acceptance and attempted apathy. Now was hardly the time to stop that over one minor assistance. A genuine act of support. Borderline heroism.

He really needed to thank Jasper.

Jasper clearly didn't want to be thanked. He was avoiding Charlie on purpose. He hadn't even set a trap for him in days. The butler was observant, if nothing else, and probably knew not to compete with Kopeck for traps. Besides, his traps were designed to humiliate and aggravate, never to hurt.

And none of this pertained to the pressing issue at hand! Unless the issue was that Charlie couldn't get out of his own way. He couldn't recover from his own buried issues enough to focus on Kopeck. There was a serial killer on the loose. Again. One who had told Charlie — had promised him — that she would get him back, that she would find a way to come after him and everyone close to him. And that was the problem: instead of heeding the warning, he'd spent years getting ever closer to more people. His days of hunting London's worst on his own were over, and now all he could think about were the people he was putting in danger.

As if on cue, footsteps sounded in the hallway. Footsteps he recognised instantly. The door creaked when it opened. Florin stood in the silhouette of the frame and watched him. Her eyes took in his position in the room, his stance and expression, the old blood on the carpet…

"I was wondering where you'd gotten yourself to," she sighed.

"I needed to think," Charlie muttered.

"Everyone in London is looking for Kopeck, Charlie," she assured, sinking slowly towards him. "If she sneezes, someone will catch her. It doesn't always have to be you."

Shilling didn't say anything. He didn't know what to say in response. What he was thinking wasn't appropriate, because it was trying to analyse what Kopeck would do. What she would say if she saw them talking. She had gone through old connections — familial connections. She had gone after Esther and then Shilling's sisters. He was lucky Rebecca was such a good hand with a poker. If he were Kopeck, he would be looking for the resources to finish what he'd started. He'd do it by whatever means necessary, and if he couldn't get to the people close to Shilling… he'd go after the adjacent innocents.

"Charlie…" Florin tried again. She reached him, placing a hand on his arm and standing altogether too close. It was the same energy with which she had embraced him in the studio. Her voice and actions imploring him equally.

The half of his brain that was still evaluating through Kopeck's eyes saw her in an entirely new light. He could see, with a detached and calculated fascination, exactly what Julian and Michael saw. Probably what everyone saw. The reason Bullion and his cronies had been especially disparaging at Harry's wake. It wasn't just obvious that Charlie floundered and gawked and pined around her, she was far too attentive towards him — even for a friend. He'd been oblivious, in truth it was deeply confusing to the part of him that was Charlie, but the part of him that was Shilling, the part that was empathising with Kopeck, was engrossed by the possibilities of her vulnerability.

Instead of shying away, he turned into her, watching as her breath caught and her pulse quickened in the hollow of her throat.

"What do you want, Florin?" he whispered, letting her catch him.

Her hand tightened on his sleeve instinctively. He moved into her space, closing the poor excuse for a gap that she'd left between them. Florin was holding her breath. He could see her chest pulled in tight behind her corset, unable to draw air into her lungs because if they expanded the two of them would be touching, her body pressed to his in the abandoned office. She made no move to back away. He raised a hand slowly, his fingers nearing the side of her face. Florin was staring at him, half-stunned and half-spellbound, like neither of them were sure if he'd actually do it. His thumb had barely brushed the edge of her cheek when a voice called for her in the corridor.

Charlie recognised the careful tones of Penny, one of the household's maids, calling tentatively for her Doctor Florin. The sound of someone who wanted to be heard before she stumbled on something she shouldn't see. The woman wasn't stupid, and Charlie finally realised that they had been obvious — to everyone but themselves.

He let go of Florin instantly, stepping away and pulling his sleeve gently from her grasp. She didn't fight him, but she didn't move either. She stood there numbly as he walked away and strode to the door, pulling it open and peering into the corridor.

"She's in here, Miss," he called, inviting Penny into the office. "Is her father looking for her?"

"Oh no, Sir, she was looking for you, and we got a message for you, so I was hoping she'd found you," Penny replied, hurrying to the doorway but stopping short of the threshold.

Florin was still standing near the desk, with the multiple lights around the walls casting shadows off her like dark flower petals. She looked shaken, and Charlie wished he had the decency to feel bad about that. It would come later, he was sure.

"You have a message for me?" he asked.

Penny ignored the question, eyeing them up with

more disapproval than just gossipy curiosity.

"You two shouldn't be in here," Penny warned carefully.

"Just double-checking old evidence," Charlie replied, not completely sure if he was lying, but feeling an awful lot like he was. He'd always prided himself on his honesty, even when Rebecca and others disapproved of just how honest he was being, and it was strangely nauseating to realise how dishonest he'd been the last few months. He'd been lying barefaced to everyone, including himself, without even realising.

Florin seemed to stir from her trance as she saw them watching her from the doorway, and she hurried from the room like she'd been caught doing something she shouldn't. She brushed by them both, pushing between them with an uncharacteristic lack of decorum. He wanted to stop her. He wanted to catch her arm, and pull her in close, and ask her what was wrong. But he knew what was wrong, and he didn't act on his instincts. He let her go without a breath or a word.

"Come along, Mister Shilling," Penny cautioned, grabbing his elbow and pulling him into the hallway. She leant over the threshold to flick the light switch off, but wouldn't enter the space, closing the door sharply behind them all. "That room's haunted," she added, taking a key from her pocket to lock it up again.

"There's no such thing," Charlie said automatically.

Penny gave him a look so severe he nearly wanted to doubt himself, but he didn't. There was no such thing as ghosts. The room was not haunted. It was a very good room, and thousands of London's poorest would be honoured to stay in a space so luxurious — whatever the history.

Or they should have been. But if the expression on Penny's face told him anything, it was that ordinary folk were dangerously superstitious. How someone who believed in hauntings was clever enough to have spotted Shilling and Florin pining over each other was the real mystery. It did not give him hope for the faint remnants of possibility that they hadn't been uncomfortably obvious.

"You said you had a message for me, Miss Penny?" he repeated, trying to get them back on track before someone else tried to lecture him on the supernatural.

"A little lad came by the back of the house and dropped it off," she nodded, pulling a scrap of paper from her pocket. "Said you'd know what it is. Looks like it could be a clue to your case." She handed it over, failing to hide a trace of excitement and curiosity at the prospect of watching him solve a murder.

Shilling unrolled the note. His eyes scanned it twice, deciphering the shorthand.

"Charlie...?" Florin queried. There was an unusual, strained hesitation in her voice. Charlie immediately hated it, and enough of him was starting to return to himself to feel horrified that he'd caused it. He knew that was his fault.

When he looked up from the note he met her eyes. Her auburn eyebrows were slanted in her dark face, but she settled as their gazes locked and she saw him in there again. He took a moment, seeing her just as she was, as he always saw her, with her forest green eyes and her black freckles, like some woodland goddess from an old faerie tale. Someone like him had no chance of startling someone like her. It felt good to put things back the right way around.

"It's from Skipp," he told her. "We need to see your father."

Florin nodded and led on. Part of him wished she had grabbed his hand and dragged him with her, the way she seemed prone to do these days, but he understood her reluctance to touch him in these halls, especially after their behaviour in the office. He was happy enough just to follow her to her father's living room, where Henry was taking tea with Susan and Rebecca.

"Where have you two been skulking?" Rebecca teased when they entered.

Susan and Henry chuckled. Charlie didn't. Florin blushed at his side and he did his best to ignore it. It felt impossible to try and treat her like any normal person, but he had to or he would end up making a mess of things.

"Pound, we just received word from Skipp's underground network," Charlie addressed Henry.

"Why do I get the impression I'm not supposed to know about that?" Henry raised an eyebrow at him.

"Someone matching Kopeck's description — down to the broken arm — was just seen buying a gun down in Southwark," Charlie relayed. "The officers looking for her need to know that she's armed and preparing to kill."

"They already know that, Shilling," Henry replied.

"No one is underestimating this woman. I can pass on the information — do you have any witnesses they can speak to?"

Charlie pulled a face, but everyone was looking at him so he tried to keep it subtle.

"The seller will be the best person to speak to, but he won't want to talk, not to cops," Charlie frowned. "He's known as 'Old Bob' and he shifts disreputable goods to disreputable people near the river in Southwark. Any constable who walks a beat near there will know who you're talking about."

"Thank you for passing this on," Henry nodded to him. "I'll make sure Farthing and the officers know."

Charlie nodded in reply. "Of course."

"It's unlike you, Shilling," Henry commented, eyeing him again. "Normally you're loath to disclose information that could help the police, choosing instead to use it yourself and run amuck through cases, leaving a trail of chaos and endangerment in your wake."

Charlie watched the room watch him. His sisters did not look in a hurry to disagree with Lord Pound. In fact, their eyes were reproving. He only recognised it because he'd spent most of his life getting that cautionary look from Rebecca. His fingers were circling his coat buttons, but he wasn't sure when it had started.

"Maybe I've had enough chaos and endangerment for one day," he murmured, silently excusing himself without permission. No one tried to stop him. Their expressions had all turned gravely sympathetic at his statement, and the silence had been uncomfortable, so he'd abandoned it.

However, he was no more than a few footsteps up the passage when Florin fell in beside him. Her expressions had not aligned with everyone else, but he had mostly been trying to ignore that. Right now, her eyes were wisely critical as she surveyed him.

"I'm sorry, Florin," he apologised to his shoes, awkwardly making his way through the house. "I just… I think I just need to rest for a bit." He said it in a way that he hoped conveyed the entirety of what he was apologising for.

"I think you do at that," she agreed with professional medical approval, and a touch of forgiveness that settled his unease.

She walked him to his room. A second of panic flickered in him that she thought to accompany him, but after the briefest of glances around his guestroom, she offered to retrieve more blankets and let him be. He opened his mouth to tell her that wasn't her job, but he didn't want her to make it someone else's job, and it made him like her more that she had no hesitations at performing menial tasks. Florin, despite her family, didn't strike Charlie as someone who had ever described any undertaking as beneath her. Perhaps it was one of the reasons he admired her so.

She brought him two extra blankets, made sure someone had stacked the wood basket by the fire, and then left him be. It made perfect sense and yet was one of the most confusing interactions of his life.

She should have slapped him for his earlier behaviour. That was almost to be expected. She had not been hesitant in her aggression in the past — when he had questioned her relationship with Harry before they had discovered his identity as the Jack, and in France when he had thought to go investigating without her to keep her from stumbling across Bonheur. Surely he was due a shakedown for this new blunder. But she said nothing. She did nothing. She acted like it hadn't happened.

That was the polite thing to do. It was the responsible thing. Thank God one of them could manage it.

Shilling investigated the bedroom window. Locked, but that wasn't a problem. The three-storey drop was. It was dark, but it wasn't late enough to stop people checking up on him. He would have to wait a little while at least.

Besides, he was genuinely exhausted. He flopped fully dressed on the bed and pulled the extra blankets over himself. Just a few minutes. Just enough time for the others to make their way to bed as well. For a moment, he was worried he might really drift off under the toll his body had taken the last few days, but it was wasted worry. His mind wouldn't let him sleep properly until the case was done. He'd learnt that lesson before.

Still, the rest was nice. It would have been nicer to stay in the studio, keep himself busy while he thought instead of lying in the dark, stewing, but his body appreciated lying there peacefully. It might have been more than an hour, but certainly less than two, when he'd heard enough people moving about the house to bed and decided the coast was clear.

It was immediately cold outside the blankets, and he snuck silently from the room. The drop from his window was too severe, but none of Pound's servants would stop him from leaving or alert his Lordship. As far as they were concerned, Charlie was an investigator who would come and go as he pleased. It was just the nobility he had to watch out for, and they were all —

Florin caught him on the second landing. He should have expected that. She'd certainly expected him. He'd snuck around the corner staircase and nearly jumped out of his skin when she stepped out of the shadows.

"Going somewhere?" she asked.

It was so cliché and he wanted to be mad about it, but he just couldn't. Of course she'd caught him. If anyone could… and she seemed to know that. She didn't demand a reply and he didn't flounder for one. He just pulled a face and she shook her head at him.

"I knew I'd find you sneaking out in the middle of the night," she rebuked.

"It's hardly the middle, Florin," he corrected. "I make it barely more than ten."

Funnily enough, his correction did nothing to improve her mood. Her eyes were severe as she out-stared him. He had done nothing to prepare himself for this. Right now, when she looked at him, it made him feel terribly weak in the knees, and he was fidgeting with his ring before he even knew he was doing it.

"I know you disapprove," he muttered at his fingers. "But I have to do this. They're not going to catch her. They didn't the first time. She messed up coming after my family, maybe she's a bit rusty after prison, but it's not enough to drop her in the hands of the police. She will hurt more people, Florin. There are always innocent bystanders that can be preyed upon. She will hurt them and leave me messages carved into their bodies if I don't stop her."

"I know," Florin nodded, patting the pockets of her full skirts. "I'm already packed."

He looked up to meet her eyes again. They were full of understanding, and he knew he didn't have to explain or justify himself. Florin knew exactly what he was doing and why he was doing it, and she wanted to help. He couldn't bring himself to turn her down. Besides, if she wasn't with him, he'd spend the whole time worrying where she was and if she was safe.

There was nothing to say, so he settled for a grateful nod as she joined him for the final flight of stairs. Her hand crept into his. He didn't comment on that either. It was tentative, but reassuring. Comforting. They were nearly at the front door when another interruption caught him in his tracks. This one manifested as a judgemental clearing of a throat.

Shilling and Florin paused at the doorway and looked back.

"Jasper…" Charlie muttered nervously.

Jasper said nothing. He lounged in the hallway down the side of the staircase, eyeing them critically through the railings. Charlie could see the bandage on his forehead from his earlier injury. He'd got that trying to protect Charlie's sisters. Surely he understood. He'd even risked his life again to save Charlie's. Charlie still hadn't said anything about it, but the way Jasper was looking at him... he didn't want Charlie to say anything. That didn't mean Jasper wouldn't. There was nothing to stop him causing a scene and being a hero again.

"Jasper, please..." Charlie implored. "We have to. It's the only way to protect Sue and Becky. It's the only way to stop her."

Jasper said nothing. He wasn't meeting Charlie's eye, but his gaze was on them. It was fixed between them, shrewd and considerate. He was staring at their clasped hands. Charlie could see him looking. He didn't let go, but he stepped carefully in front of Florin to hide the object of Jasper's curiosity. Jasper's eyes flicked up to him, finally meeting his gaze with a tight resignation. He was letting them go. Charlie could see it in his expression. He wasn't going to tell.

"Thank you, Jasper," he whispered. "Truly, thank you."

"Charles..." Jasper sighed, barely looking at him anymore. "Just... be careful."
Charlie nodded. It felt like the longest sincere conversation they'd had in six years, and Charlie didn't want to wait for Jasper to change his mind. The instant he knew he was safe, he tightened his grip on Florin's hand, fled out the door, and stole away into the night.

10

The night was dark and cold, and Amy was half expecting rain. It hadn't hit yet. They had crossed the river into Southwark and headed down towards the docks. It was a dim and dismal area near the bridge, where crime and poverty hoped to make the most of unguarded ships.

Charlie walked like he knew the area well. Amy was grateful for his hand in hers, holding her tightly and keeping her close. She knew he was rattled. Something wasn't right. Something old and awful was stirring in him at having to deal with Kopeck again. But she felt like she understood that. That fear and guilt… she understood how natural that could be. She remembered how she'd felt when she'd realised who the Jack of Hearts had been… and why he'd killed. She knew what it was to feel guilty for lives taken by hands that weren't even her own.

Her other hand was tucked safe and warm in her pocket, resting lightly on the handle of her father's pistol hidden deep in her skirts. That gun was the same weapon she had drawn on Harry to stop him killing Charlie at her graduation event. She had a horrible feeling she was going to need it to stop Kopeck killing

Charlie as well. How he had ever managed to survive his cases without her, she had no idea.

How this had become her life, she also had no idea. She had lived through every moment, and it was still surreal. Harry, Argent and Bonheur, now this…

Life with Charlie Shilling was stranger than fiction. She couldn't help but imagine what Laura and Jane would say if they could see her now. They would be furious, or at the very least admonishing. She could practically see Jane's serious glare, her whispered accusations of 'are you out of your mind?!'. Laura would be looking at her with those giant dark eyes, a concerned pout in her cute round face, going 'Oh darling, you know we love and support you, but this…?'

But she was helping to track down a killer. Again. She was keeping Charlie safe. She had to. The cases she'd worked with him had proven the genius to be a bit hopeless on his own.

Even as she thought it, she was caught off guard. The sights and smells and sounds of the world beneath the bridge were disorientating. Sailors and scoundrels gathered around bin fires, but the glowing flames only served to deepen the shadows, and the smoke only added to the smog. The stench of the river was noxious, and the sounds of the docks echoed and bounced until you could never quite be sure where some noises came from out of the haze.

A man stepped out of the shadows, pulling a knife on them. Amy hadn't even heard him approach. He grinned a gap-toothed grin behind a scraggly beard, violence in his bloodshot eyes.

"Now, wha' are two cute kids like you doing 'round here?" His words stank of whisky and halitosis.

Amy tightened her hand on the pistol, but she never drew it from her pocket. She barely saw him move. She felt the immediate chill of Charlie's hand leaving hers. Then a scuffle. She felt like all she did was blink and suddenly Charlie was standing over the other man. Their would-be assailant was half-crumpled on the ground. Charlie had him by the collar in one hand, and the other hand pressed the man's own knife to his throat. The man was groaning and gasping like he'd been stunned. He blinked owlishly up at Charlie in a drunken haze.

"Shilling...?" he muttered.

"Hello Bob," Charlie replied, still holding the man down.

Bob grinned wolfishly at him. "Charlie-boy! I didn't even recognise you with such a handsome lady on your arm! What are you doing here?"

"We're here to have a chat with you, Bob," Charlie told him.

"Always a pleasure, lad," Bob grinned his gappy grin. "Come have a drink."

"Sorry Bob," Charlie sighed, slowly letting go of the man's coat and letting him slump. "We might not have time for that tonight. Got a few questions. Urgent questions."

"I got nicer stuff, if you need to impress your girl," Bob suggested conspiratorially. "What happened? You workin' her case? She got a runner?"

"She's not a House Lady, she's a doctor," Charlie smiled at him. He flipped the knife in his hand and offered it back to its owner, handle first. "Knows how to cut you up and stitch you back together."

Bob shot her an appropriately impressed and intimidated look. Charlie knew how to make it sound like more than it was.

"And Bob," he added, his eyes never leaving the slumped felon, "she's not happy to see you, Bob. That is a gun in her pocket. So we're going to be polite to the nice doctor, aren't we?"

Bob huffed a chuckle, eyeing them both.

"Aye, shoulda known with you, Shilling. Shoulda known..." He heaved himself to his feet, swaying slightly.

Amy watched them both, trying to hide her surprise that Charlie knew about the pistol. She hadn't told him. She thought she'd been hiding it, but there must have been a tell. Knowing him, it could have been the slightest thing. His observational skills were infamous, after all. He wasn't even watching her. He hadn't looked to her at all since Bob had appeared. He seemed to have his eyes firmly locked on the old crook, but she knew better than to believe he didn't have the entire area perceived and evaluated.

Bob pocketed his knife and drew out a battered old flask. He took a hearty swig from it and held it out invitingly.

"Sure I can't tempt you...?" he coaxed.

"Not tonight," Charlie smiled tightly.

Bob held the flask out to Amy and she shook her

head. It was kind of him to include her, she supposed, but whatever was in that flask no one could pay her to try it. Bob draped an arm around Shilling, smiling with drunken fondness.

"He's a good lad, this one," Bob told her like he was selling something. "Me and Shilling, we're made of the same stuff — good sorts, call 'em like we see 'em. He's got a keen eye too. Sharp as a tack, quick as a fox, and fearless enough to piss on the Queen — God spit in her eye."

A wry smile twisted Charlie's lopsided mouth. Amy watched stoically. It wasn't news to her that Charlie got on with people like this. It was a huge part of why he used to fight so much with her father, and why the papers always swung between admiring his genius and vilifying his politics.

That was when she noticed it. Really noticed it. The set of his jaw and the tightness around his eyes. Charles Shilling. Professional sleuth. Amateur scoundrel. There was a difference between detective Shilling and Charlie, like two separate people. Shilling was the genius and the ruffian. He could spot a crime a mile away and shakedown the necessary parties for answers and clues. But he wasn't her Charlie. Or he was, but not like she knew him. At his heart, she knew Charlie lay as confused and lost as any other person, but Shilling had mastered unflappability and ruthlessness.

Charlie had humanity. He had been helping Florin ever since she had discovered the truth about the Jack. She had needed him and he had obliged. He had offered her the raggedy and harmless side of himself like a token of friendship and she had gobbled it up desperately. Now she was still following him around greedily, hoping for more.

There wasn't more.

Worse, Charlie had been put back in the box.

Shilling had stepped out to deal with Kopeck. Charlie had nearly gotten himself killed trying to take care of Amy while stopping the Jack; had nearly gotten himself skewered in France trying to help Amy help her parents. Charlie couldn't afford to risk being what she needed anymore. Not this time. This time he had to choose competence over kindness.

But she missed her Charlie.

Except… he wasn't really her Charlie. She had no more claim to him than she had to Bob. He was a person like any other, and it wasn't his fault she had falsely and unfairly romanticised him.

"Bob," Shilling addressed the drunk. "Earlier tonight you sold a gun to a woman with a broken arm. I need to know everything you can tell me about her, the weapon, and where I can find her."

"Y'know, Charlie-boy, I'm not really sure—" Bob began, scratching his beard.

"I have absolutely no time to fuck around, Robert," Charlie cut him off coolly.

Bob flinched and he wasn't the only one. Amy pressed her lips together nervously, trying to calm her racing heart. She'd never seen Shilling like this. There was a hardness in his eyes that Bob was cowering from, like he was actually afraid of scruffy little Charlie Shilling. But he was right to be scared, and Amy felt like she was having a heart attack watching the revelation unfold.

Shilling kept his grey eyes on the drunken crook, his gaze steely and unyielding. Bob slouched back against the stone pylon, but there was nowhere to go and no way he was getting anywhere faster than Shilling. A nervous frown crinkled behind his beard. Loose strands of Charlie's messy straw hair fell across his eyes and he smoothed them back patiently, his temperament clear in his voice and somehow all the more chilling.

"You met her, Bob, and you're still alive," Shilling said. "That means she ripped you off and you're grateful she did, because it didn't cost you your liver. You need your liver, Bob. Not going to get very far if she cuts it from your squealing body."

"You don't wanna find her, Shilling," Bob muttered anxiously. "Don't do this. She'll gut you."

"I caught her once, I can do it again," Shilling replied.

"She's..." Bob trailed off in terror, casting glances around like he was worried someone was listening. There was no one else close enough, but he still shook his head and clamped his jaw.

"She's a psychopath," Shilling nodded. "Believe me, Bob, I know. What's more, she wants me to find her. She cut up a little girl to get my attention. Now, tell me where she's hiding. I know you know."

Bob seemed to weigh this up. He was clearly reluctant, but Shilling was the unstoppable force to his immovable object, and the object was cracking. Amy wasn't sure if it was fear of Shilling or a flare of conscience, but Bob's unwillingness seemed to settle into bitter resignation.

"She's comin' up for air in the East End," he muttered. "I don't know more, lad. I don't want to."

Shilling gave him a wry, lopsided smile, barely more than a grimace, but he patted Bob's shoulder gratefully.

"At least don't get the nice lady tangled up in it!" Bob protested, waving his flask at Amy in one last desperate attempt to talk them out of it. "She ain't got what it takes for this."

"Anything I can do, she can do better. She's worth two of me," Shilling smirked. "She's allowed to make her own decisions, Bob. I ain't gonna tell her what to do."

"You're gonna get yourself killed, Charlie-boy," Bob sighed miserably, taking a swig from his flask. "Streets'll be sadder without ya."

Charlie looked like he was about to say something, but seemed to think better of it. Bob took another sad slurp, his drinking getting noisier.

"You're one of the few, lad..." Bob muttered. "One of the few. We know there's no God, no justice, but you always been delusional. Chasing devils." Bob shifted against the pylon, making himself comfortable against the stone, and sinking like a turtle back into his coat.

"Nothing's real, Bob," Shilling sighed, digging a few coins out and slipping them into his informant's coat pocket. "God and justice are just the same as everything else — as real as we make them." He gave the man another pat on the arm and Bob nodded gratefully for the coins. Then Shilling stepped away from him, nodded his head to Amy, and led her off to cross back over the river.

11

Shilling was waiting for his anger to outweigh his fear. It felt like it was going to be a long wait. The biggest problem he faced was that Kopeck was hiding in the tunnels, and everyone knew about it, even the police were down there looking, but he couldn't follow. The very thought of trying began to tighten his chest and constrict his breathing. He needed his desperation to catch Kopeck to beat his fears of being buried alive again. Surely that couldn't be hard.

But it was, and it was getting harder.

New fears kept springing into life. As he led Florin into the East End slums, Bob's words gained substance. Florin, for all her magnificence, or perhaps because of it, shouldn't be here. The only reason she was trailing along was because of him. This wasn't her fight. The thoughts slowed him in his tracks. She stopped when he stopped.

"Florin," he turned to her anxiously, "it's not too late to turn back. I know you're more than capable, but Kopeck is... well, she's... I don't want..."

"Shilling," she cut off his weak excuses. "I'm not here to mess about. I'm here to make sure you get it done this time. I'm not leaving here until we have

Kopeck in custody, and if that involves a few bullets to her knees… she should have thought of that before she hurt that little girl."

Shilling blinked at her. He felt like he'd been slapped, and it wouldn't have been the first time Florin had knocked sense into him, but this time she'd done it with words and… and they stung. They stung extra because… because she'd called him Shilling. He remembered when she had made the switch to Charlie, and it had felt so informal, but… but he'd liked it. He'd grown used to it. There was a softness in the way she said his name, an affection he had silently clung to.

That had not been present in her voice when she had called him Shilling. He appreciated her sentiment and her anger. He knew exactly how she felt in that regard. The tragic fate of Esther was enough to drive anyone mad. But… not his Amy.

He swallowed thickly, trying to find the words to respond. Before he could summon the eloquence, she turned away dismissively, as though ensuring he couldn't continue his argument.

The streets were crowded tonight in the Old Nichol Street Rookery, but the energy was hushed and anxious. Florin moved to a group of people huddled in a doorway and began to make inquiries. Shilling watched her work. He'd half expected her to struggle down here, the way he did when he had to communicate with her society. It wasn't the same. He couldn't talk to the upper echelon because he couldn't respect anyone who thought they were born better than someone else. Florin was a doctor, she knew how to talk to everyone, and she knew how to do so respectfully. She'd probably done a lot of charity work in conditions like this during her studies. It was optional, but she seemed like the type.

It made him love her more, he admitted in absolute and unspoken privacy. When she rolled up her sleeves, he had heart palpitations. Florin checked the fever of a child in the crowd and began rummaging in her pockets. Shilling wondered if he could use the distraction to sneak off and follow the rather wide trail of breadcrumbs that had been exposing itself while he stood there. Except he couldn't take his eyes off her.

"That you, Mister Shilling?" a voice sounded behind him. He turned as a woman in a filthy apron and ragged headscarf approached him. "Gee, you got here quick."

"You been expecting me?" he grimaced.

The woman gave him a look like she knew he knew, and he just nodded. The lady stopped at his side. She moved with a limp that spoke of blisters and favoured her right foot when she stood. He turned his attention back to Amy.

"Good work on the Jack though," the lady complimented him. "S'pose that's his bird, then? We heard you've been keeping her company."

"We're colleagues," he replied with a stunningly convincing apathy that surprised him. "Her medical expertise is extremely useful."

The lady didn't even scoff or roll her eyes. It was a refreshing change. Of course, all they got down here were the dregs of gossip. Most of them weren't literate enough to read Tanner's rubbish, thankfully. Unfortunately, he wasn't doing his story any favours.

Florin was crouched in the doorway, looking at a mark on someone's arm. Another person held a candle closer for her to see by. She motioned the light nearer and it backlit her like a halo. The glow highlighted her curls and accentuated the red in her hair. She looked like an angel.

Charlie just stared. He knew everyone could see, and he knew he had a terrible poker face, but he had a terrible everything face, and this was hardly the most dire issue in his life right now.

"You're not takin' her with you?" the lady asked sceptically.

Charlie's heart broke. He wanted to say no. He wanted more than anything to say no, but God herself couldn't stop Amy from chasing him into danger — he certainly didn't know how to. He looked to the woman at his side, trying to convey the situation with his eyes. She seemed to understand. Her expression conveyed her pity, and a slight jerk of her head was the best advice he could get.

He turned and walked quickly up the street. It was the only reasonable solution he had. His best chance was to disappear into the crowds and follow them back to the street where they thinned tellingly. In this part of town, people weren't picky — you made do with what you had, and you did the best with it that you could.

At the end of the road stood a small gothic church. It looked haunted. That people had abandoned it, even for one night, was telling. He didn't think people around here avoided church for the same reasons he did. Obviously, something else was afoot. Something to do with a serial killer who would be pushing people out and looking for new prey, while also basing herself somewhere with excellent access to the tunnels — like a crypt.

He headed down the street, his eyes on the building, scouring for any sign of life or danger. This was a part of town Kopeck had done a decent portion of her business in before Shilling had caught her. Her kidnapping business, that was. Lots of children had gone missing around here when she had been loose. He shouldn't have been surprised she'd come back. People in these parts would still be too scared to stand up to her. It had only been five, maybe six, years ago. Not enough time for the fear to die off.

Shilling stopped outside the church, loitering in the shadows and cocking his head to the side as he regarded it. Only way in was going to be through the main doors. Obvious trap. Windows were already boarded, even the stained glass. Someone had taken the time to fortify that place. That was why everyone in the street knew, why they'd been expecting him. They knew she was laying a trap for him, and they weren't going to cross her to stop it.

He stood and considered the situation. Suddenly, a hand slipped into his. He should have spooked, but he wasn't surprised. Maybe he'd known. Maybe he'd heard her approach, or smelt her perfume a moment before she'd arrived. Her fingers interlaced with his and squeezed.

"You are an absolute baked trout, Charlie Shilling," she told him witheringly.

He wasn't quite sure how that was an insult, but her tone gave him no room to doubt that it was. Perhaps she meant he was flaky. Couldn't fault her for that. Couldn't fault himself for trying though. He turned to look at her, and found her watching him with damning green eyes from a dark face of black freckles. Those eyes understood, but they were cold.

"I don't want you to get hurt," he explained, finding the words so much easier now that she was already angry. They still came out in a muted whisper, like he was worried the universe would hear them and see it as a challenge. Florin squeezed his hand again, harder this time.

"I know exactly how you feel," she replied, and there was absolutely nothing he could do with that.

This must have been exactly how Rebecca and Michael felt all these years. He couldn't do anything to stop Florin from throwing herself into danger, the same way they'd never been able to stop him. Besides, he and Florin had come too far together now. If he'd really wanted to ditch her, he would have had to do it at the house. That had been when he'd caved, and it was too late to pretend otherwise.

"It's a trap," he warned her.

"I know," she replied. "But it's a trap for you. Not me."

"You think you can beat her?" he asked.

"I think we have to try," she answered. "If we call the police, Kopeck will spook and a lot of officers could die. I think that's why you always try to do these things alone."

He gave that an acquiescing nod.

"But I think she's in there expecting you, and I think that gives us an element of surprise," Florin finished.

"I hope you're right," Shilling muttered. She squeezed his hand again, this time like she might never let it go.

"I'm not going to let anything happen to you, Charlie," she promised.

He looked to her, but she was watching the church now and wouldn't meet his eye. She'd called him Charlie again. He didn't understand what the change meant. He hadn't understood the previous times either. He only knew how to observe that there was a change and that it had meaning.

He knew that wasn't enough.

But there wasn't time for more. He couldn't ask her to explain it, and they had done more than enough standing around.

"If we could get into the tunnels, we could get at her from below..." he mused. "She won't be expecting that."

Florin gave him a look like she already knew he couldn't do it. Shilling grimaced. It was the best way — the smartest way — but... but he just couldn't. Florin wasn't wrong and she did know. She could, undoubtedly, feel his hand start to tremble in her grasp the more he thought about it.

"There'll be a back door," she assured him.

"She will have bolted that up as well," he grumbled. "I guess we're just going to have to do this the hard way."

"Do you know any other way of doing things?" Florin teased him.

He glowered and did not dignify the joke with a response. Besides, she'd just have another witty retort ready if he tried, and then he'd be hopelessly undone by that. He could spend all night getting entranced by Florin's sense of humour, but if Kopeck thought she'd lost him or that he couldn't find her, she'd make sure there were the screams of another child for him to follow. He couldn't live with that. Instead, he led Florin to the church, and they snuck carefully and quietly to the door.

She let his hand go as he crouched to pick the lock. He missed the comfort of the gesture, but they weren't out here to play nice. He needed to work. The lock wasn't difficult and he popped it quickly. Florin reached for the handle. He snatched her wrist tightly. She paused. They shared a look. It was too close to the building to risk speaking. Kopeck might hear them. Shilling shook his head warningly. Florin moved her hand back and Shilling let her go.

He took a small pen knife from his pocket and moved to the hinges, carefully prying the pins loose and indicating to Florin to help him hold the door in place. She gave him a strange look, but did as he asked. Each hinge pin was carefully wedged free and pocketed, then Shilling got Florin to help him tip the door carefully inward.

Sure enough, Shilling could see through the gap where the string tied to the inner door handle went slack. It was attached to what appeared to be a carefully rigged gunpowder device. He used the knife to cut the string cautiously from the doorhandle, before it could pull the pin on the deadly contraption. With that sorted, the two of them gently set the door aside, out of the way. Shilling dug through his pockets, pulling out a few scraps of paper.

Florin gave him a questioning look, followed by a slight crinkle of disgust along her nose as he chewed one up (an old receipt) and used the wet paper to jam the pin in place. He cut the rest of the string off it too, just in case.

"Charlie, that's filthy!" she rebuked in a whisper, casting her eyes about but seeing no sign of anyone around to hear her.

"Blowing up's worse," he whispered back. "And I don't have any gum on me."

"How'd you know to do it?" she asked.

"Kopeck's the sort to leave traps," he muttered, disarming it as best he could and looking around. "Besides, Jasper keeps me well practiced, although he strives for humiliation rather than murder."

Shilling looked around the church. Kopeck's bomb had been set up on the font of holy water just inside the door of the porch. From here, the nave stretched all the way up to the pulpit, flanked by rows of pews. There didn't look to be anyone else inside. Shilling felt his throat tighten as he looked around. This place felt so familiar, although he was certain he'd never been here. Churches could be like that sometimes. Seen one and you'd seen them all. Except… except this one really did remind him of his father's parish. He could almost picture his small, childhood self causing chaos and digging around in the walls for evidence of God.

Where was she now?

The thought was inevitable. It always came crawling when he thought of his father. Nothing the old man had ever taught him had been able to compare with the profound lack of observable evidence. There was a murderer on the loose, a dead child, a terrified city, and a church had been rigged into a death trap. Where was God now? Was she watching?

Charlie could imagine a faceless figure in robes, seated in the front row of a theatre, snacking on roasted chestnuts, and watching the events unfold across a stage. Riveting. He'd be compelled himself, if it wasn't his life on the line.

He motioned for Florin to stay close as he stepped carefully from the porch and snuck down the side aisle. The last thing he wanted was the two of them getting separated. They moved as silently as they could across the wooden floor. Shilling was used to walking softly and he cringed inwardly at any light footstep or creak Florin made behind him. There was no helping it. He wouldn't leave her anywhere she might get hurt. Hopefully Kopeck was too preoccupied to hear the approach. If she was even here. If he'd set a trap like that one, he would not have waited around to watch it go off. At least, not anywhere close. Still, Kopeck was a psychopath. Even if she wasn't in the building, she would be close enough to watch him burn.

His initial instinct had been to sweep the entire ground floor first, but a smear on a nearby doorhandle caught his eye. He snuck to the side door, eyeing the greasy mark and sniffing gently. Gunpowder. She'd been through here after making her trap. He took the handle between his thumb and forefinger, careful to dodge the smudge, and turned it tentatively. Unlocked.

Shilling and Florin shared a look. He carefully pushed the door open into a small side corridor with stairs leading up and down. Upstairs would lead to the mezzanine, upper cloisters, and steeple. Good locations to watch the trap ignite, potentially. Downstairs would lead to the basement and the crypt. And the crypt would lead to the tunnels. Charlie steeled himself and took a deep breath.

They crept down the stairs as silently as possible. Shilling could smell it before he saw it. Gunpowder and blood. The door to the basement was ajar and light spilled out from it. He snuck to the entrance and peered through the crack. Someone had been working in there. Possibly they still were. It didn't make sense to leave the room unchecked. He told himself that on repeat, insisting that was the reason to stay here and abandon the descent, ignoring the part of his brain that was begging him not to go any deeper underground.

He pushed the door open further with the side of his boot. It drifted slowly and silently. His eyes scanned the room like a hawk, picking up every little detail. There was a lot of blood on the floor. Someone had died in here, although it wasn't immediately obvious who. Probably the vicar, Shilling thought sickly. The spread and quantity of the puddle suggested an adult. The body had since been dragged and then carried from the room.

The basement was a massive chamber, but the loadbearing nature of the construction divided it into smaller spaces. They weren't properly cordoned off rooms. It was more that the illusion of walls had been created by frequent pillars and beams, and then heavily reinforced by excessive storage. The source of the light was a single workstation, well-lit. It did not look like it belonged to anyone who worked at the church.

He couldn't get a good look from there, so snuck carefully into the room. Florin followed close behind, right on his tail. She drew her pistol, holding it nervously at the ready. They stepped carefully around the pool of blood. Florin kept her eyes on the room, watching Shilling's back. He stalked to the workstation. The remains of the bomb's construction were strewn about, along with various bits and bobs, and a strange assortment of diaries and newspaper clippings.

Charlie recognised them. Even just a glance told him what they were, but he couldn't help but flick through the neatly cut stacks of articles. They were about him. With the exception of a few, which clearly tied back to Kopeck's own work, the clippings were all stories about him. His past cases. Some of them were even reputable. They went back years… five at least. Kopeck's case was here. There was a small article from his early days about the oddball brother-in-law of Lady Guinea who had started taking private work on missing persons cases. That was what had set him on Kopeck's trail to begin with.

The last stack, sitting prominent from the rest, were

the Shilling and Florin articles. Everything since the Jack. Some of them were newsworthy. Most of them were Tanner's. There was a new one Shilling hadn't seen before, neatly sliced out on top. Harry's funeral. Apparently, Amelia Florin had caused a scene with her new lover at her fiancé's funeral — possibly due to guilt for what she and Shilling had done to Harry. According to the article, evidence suggested (but was not specified or supplied, Charlie noted) that Pound Junior had been driven to suicide by reports of Shilling and Florin's elopement to Paris. That printed turd of an article was sitting beneath this one. Charlie noted Lionel took no responsibility for the damage his stories might have caused, even if any of his nonsense about Harry's death happened to be true.

Charlie ground his teeth in bitter frustration. If Lord Pound didn't get the catchpenny with libel, Charlie was going to get Julian to hang him upside down in his own chimney and leave him there. It was nothing less than the tabloid-snake deserved.

A sound caught his ear. Too distant to be Florin. Shilling moved instantly. He stepped back, catching Florin around the waist and pulling her back with him behind a stack of crates. A gunshot cracked through the room and a hail of splinters exploded above them. Less than a second between sounds. Charlie eyed the distance and cover to the exit, calculating their odds. Florin shoved him down, crouching around the crates and firing her pistol. Charlie heard the bullet hit wood. More splintering. Too solid a sound for another crate. Must have been a pillar. Maybe a beam? He tried to measure the angle Florin was firing at, but she had her knee pressed into his side to keep him down.

"Predictable as ever, Mister Shilling," Kopeck's voice echoed through the basement. "Disarm a trap, follow a couple of clues… you get a few wins, and you think yourself ahead. You think yourself superior."

Another shot sounded. The lamps exploded and darkness fell. A bang echoed in the room. The door shutting.

"You are easy to trap, little mouse," Kopeck mocked.

In the darkness, the oppressive weight of the building above seemed to quadruple. As though the basement were deeper. As though it were miles underground… about to cave in. Shilling tried to steady his breathing. He could hear Kopeck's footsteps coming closer.

"Florin," he whispered as quietly as possible. He could still feel her near. She leant closer to his voice. He slipped his arms around her, following the fabric of her sleeves, and placed his hands over hers around the gun, aiming carefully. Her curls were soft against his cheek as she leant against him in the dark. The scent of her perfume filled his nose and calmed his nerves. His resolve steadied.

He might have been easy to trap, but Kopeck had never tangled with both of them before. He could still hear their adversary approaching. The footsteps were muffled and echoey. Shilling tightened his grip on Florin's, aimed according to memory, and fired.

The bullet caught the gunpowder and shrapnel across the desk. It sparked and lit. Fire caught the edges of the newspaper clippings. Shilling watching with some satisfaction as the paper caught and began to burn. Light flared across the space, illuminating their immediate surroundings and intensifying the shadows.

Kopeck appeared out of the darkness. She was huge, at least 6'5", and her ragged clothes were tight over her muscular frame. One arm was bound in a makeshift sling, but her eyes were wide with madness and reflected the fire like Satan's own gaze. She raised her pistol.

Shilling and Florin bolted. They dove in opposite directions, scattering her targets and rushing for new cover. Bullets split the crates behind them. Shilling swore he could feel them go by. Heat tickled his neck. His ears popped. The sound of the air displacing threw off his senses. He raced towards the door. The distance was too great. He dove behind a cabinet, pulling the penknife from his pocket and flicking it open. Silently, he slid down into a crouch, waiting. He just needed her to get close enough. He just needed her to go after him.

And she would.

Kopeck could be predictable too.

Shilling eyed the distance between the cabinet and a dusty stack of boxes. He was gasping as silently as he could. The light was growing in the room, so was the heat. That meant less oxygen too. He blinked sweat from his eyes and wiped his face with his sleeve. If he tried to catch her with a mirror, she'd see it. He was only going to have one shot at this, and he wasn't going to have long to measure it.

He moved slowly and silently out of cover, lining up

his throw. She was looking around for him. He raised his arm. She glimpsed the movement out of the corner of her eye. Shilling threw the blade end over end and dove behind the boxes. A grunt told him he'd got her. Not enough to stop her. She fired. Dust and paper exploded over him from the boxes. He scrambled to his feet and ran. Kopeck was chasing him. He abandoned his tactic for the door and vanished deeper under the church.

Maybe Florin could get out. Maybe, if he coaxed Kopeck down here, Florin could get to the door. She could get help, even just escape. He staggered from cover to cover, trying to mask his panting. He could hear Kopeck following. She was moving slowly, but her pace was steady. Unrelenting. Shilling knew this feeling. He knew what it was to be hunted.

The flames from the desk were beginning to lick up the walls. Shilling could see the fire growing across the room. If he didn't get back to the door, things were going to get worse fast. But if he did try and get back, and Kopeck was guarding it, she would gun him down.

Gunfire sounded behind him.

Shilling turned and ran. He didn't even think. If Kopeck was shooting and it wasn't at him, that meant Florin.

But it was Florin who'd taken the shot.

Shilling saw her down the line. She was hiding behind one of the pillars. Her curls were coming loose around her face and she was pressed back against the pillar, chest heaving and ash on her cheek. Both hands held her gun at the ready. She'd shot at Kopeck and ducked for cover. Charlie caught her eye. He gave her a reassuring nod and crept towards her.

Laughter sounded near the door. Cold, cruel laughter. Charlie grimaced at the sound. He could hear it coming closer. It was drifting towards Florin.

"So, it's true, little mouse?" Kopeck taunted. "I couldn't believe what I read in the papers… until I saw it with my own eyes. You? With a woman?" Kopeck laughed again. She stepped lightly, but her boots creaked on the floor. "I have a better chance of seducing a woman than you, Shilling."

Charlie privately agreed with that, but he also didn't think it relevant. Besides, was Kopeck really stupid enough to believe Lionel's ramblings? Maybe he'd given her intelligence too much credit. She might have broken out of prison, but she'd been studying his life and she hadn't worked out that he and Florin were just partners.

He glanced at Florin again as both he and Kopeck slowly converged on her position. The firelight made her hair redder than normal. Almost coppery. She was looking at the ceiling and he couldn't catch her eye. The flames were at the beams now. He had to get her out of here. She was only here because…

Charlie stared at her pained face in the firelight, her beautiful round cheeks, and her wild hair, and desperate eyes. She was here because they were more than partners. Because she was his friend. She was his friend and she didn't want him getting hurt. Was it really more than Michael or Julian would have done if he'd asked?

But that was the point. He hadn't asked. He hadn't had to ask. It didn't matter what he said, she wouldn't let him walk into trouble alone. She was hiding in the burning basement of an abandoned church, gun in hand, ready to kill someone, just to help keep him safe.

And Kopeck was striding forward, pistol raised, pointed at the pillar Amy hid behind as the shadows of the flames betrayed her.

"I'm going to make you watch while I flay her alive," Kopeck grinned.

Shilling charged. He shoved a stack of boxes, knocking them towards Kopeck. They crashed towards her like dominos. He lunged around the debris. Perhaps, years ago, he might have been above taking Kopeck's bait. But this was Amy. She'd threatened Amy.

Charlie leapt around the mess, grappling for Kopeck's gun. He missed, smacking her across the broken arm. He could see a bloody mark in her shoulder where his knife must have struck earlier. She grunted and kicked him full in the ribs. He hit the ground hard, but anger made him bounce. He was on his feet in a second, teeth bared and ready to strike. Kopeck raised her gun.

She'd known it was bait.

Charlie paused as he saw the shot coming. Whatever else he had doubted, he had to give Kopeck credit for that. Perhaps she had been right. After all, she'd known his weakness better than he had. He realised his hands were raised, but in retaliation or surrender, even he wasn't sure.

"Well played, Lubov," he conceded.

She smiled as she steadied her shaking hand and squeezed the trigger.

"CHARLIE!"

He was waiting for the bullet, but the sound of his name hit him first. He felt her crash into him from the side. Two shots sounded. He hit the ground with Amy on top of him.

Then the world exploded.

Kopeck's bomb went off in the atrium. He wrapped his arms around Amy, burying her face in his shoulder and covering her head with his hands. The whole building shook. The ceiling caved in. The floor buckled. It sounded like a storm. Like the inside of a shipwreck tearing apart at the seams.

The whole building shuddered and creaked. Half the basement was already on fire. Charlie felt the floor start to give way. He held Amy tighter, like somehow he could protect her from the collapsing church around them.

"I've got you," he whispered, but even like this it was inaudible amongst the explosions.

The floor collapsed and they fell. Charlie grunted as they smashed into the top of a sarcophagus in the crypt below. The sloped and broken floorboards beneath him broke some of his fall. He hoped he broke most of hers. Burning church rained down around them. He rolled away as fast as his aching body would allow, dragging Amy with him in his arms. They collapsed onto the floor of the crypt. Charlie rolled off her and clambered up, looking around. His ears were ringing and he could barely stand. The whole world seemed to be swaying.

"Kopeck?!" he bellowed into the chaos.

Half the basement was down here with them, and the crypt already looked like it had been raided. Multiple tombs were broken open, revealing dark passages. Of course. At least three tunnels into the depths of London. No wonder Kopeck had set up her base here. He couldn't see any sign of her. She hadn't come down with them. The floor of the basement sloped, half-collapsed above them. It blocked the door to the staircase. If he wanted to get back up there, he would have to climb.

"Come on, Florin," he panted, staggering dizzyingly. "I'm not letting her escape me again." He crashed into some of the splintered floorboards, hanging vertically from the rafters. Everything was spinning. He pushed off the wood, feeling it slip beneath his fingers. His hand was slippery. He paused, blinking. Everything stank of smoke. The world was hazy. His fingers were red. Blood. He looked down. There was blood on his shirt. He poked it. Just blood. He looked back.

Florin was still lying where he'd left her. He hadn't noticed against the black dress. She was still in mourning black. Her side was soaked. She was struggling to breathe.

"AMY!" he screamed, rushing back and collapsing to his knees at her side.

With one shaking hand she tried to keep pressure on her wound. Charlie clutched at it, pressing firmly at the bullet wound as it leaked between their fingers.

"Charlie…" she grimaced, wincing to draw breath. With her other hand, she fumbled the gun into his grasp. "Get h-her. Finish this. I… I can't—"

"Amy!" He clasped her cheek, ignoring her orders.

"I can't get back up there," she gasped. "N-not like this. Not w-without stairs… Y-you have to…"

"I'm getting you out of here," he promised, pocketing the gun and trying to scoop her carefully off the ground.

She cried out in pain and shook her head.

"I can't do it, Charlie," she pleaded. "I can't climb—"

"We're not climbing," he grunted, forcing her trembling hands to keep pressure on her wound as he pulled her up and supported her. He held her tightly, clutched in his arms, as they pointed towards the dark tunnels.

"No, Charlie—" she gasped, leaning against the broken sarcophagus. "Y-you can't—"

"I can," he replied. "Amy," he touched her face again, forcing her pained eyes to meet his, "I'm getting you out of here."

She grunted in pain, too hurt to speak. He pulled her tighter into his arms, steeled himself, and carried her into the darkness.

12

Waiting rooms were where souls went to die. Bodies died on operating tables, or in hospital beds, or anywhere, really. But souls… souls died waiting. Floundering, desperate, helpless. Charlie was still half-dressed, his own cuts and scrapes stitched, cleaned, and bandaged. He hadn't felt a thing. He hadn't felt a thing since they'd gotten out of the tunnels. He didn't know how long they'd been down there for. Amy had still been alive when he'd pulled her up the ladder into the street. She'd still been alive when he had screamed down a cart to take them to hospital. She'd still been alive when they'd wheeled her into the operating room.

The place bodies went to die.

Charlie had let someone else stitch him up. Apparently, it was a bad look to have him dripping blood on the waiting room floor. Worse had happened to that floor, he was certain. Now no one would talk to him. Florin was in surgery. That was all they would say. People had come and gone from this room. Charlie remained, shirt unbuttoned, numb to the cold, reeking of antiseptic alcohol.

Someone else came in. He recognised the footsteps. Someone familiar. He turned to demand answers off yet another doctor, and stopped dead. For some horrible reason, he flashed back to the morgue. Henry Pound had looked exactly the same then. Same hat, same cloak, same cane, same grey face in a pillar of mourning black, like a man hovering on the edge of life.

And Charlie was the same too. Same filthy mess. Blood and ash and tears all over his clothes. Guilt and anguish and shame constricting his heart, squeezing his brain and lungs like a snake trying to devour him alive — or whatever was left of him. There wasn't much left now, but whatever still lived in him shuddered when it saw Henry. Charlie felt his breath stop and his eyes sting, and he froze completely still, as though maybe there was a chance Pound couldn't see him if he didn't move. Except Henry was looking right at him. His eyes were taking in the state Charlie was in, his injuries and trauma and grief. Pound's lips tightened and his sideburns quivered, and Charlie felt like his whole body was going to dissolve at the sight of it. His knees buckled, still half-risen from his chair.

"Keep your seat, Charles," Henry bid him, his voice softer than Charlie had ever heard it.

Charlie did as he was told, if only because his knees collapsed beneath him. He sank back into his chair, trembling. Henry walked further into the room. Every slow step accompanied by the tap of his cane. He stopped partway down the aisle, once he was in line with Charlie. Charlie wanted to puke from guilt, but his chest was too tight for anything to get out.

"Is she…?" Henry began.

"No one will tell me anything," Charlie whispered.

He stared dead ahead, like he was happy to sit there and watch paint dry on the far wall.

Henry watched the same patch of wall. It was an off-white. An eggshell blue-grey. No marks. Regularly cleaned. His mouth twitched several times, tightening into small frowns that trembled apart and then constricted back up.

Charlie could feel his knees knocking together. His hands were quivering like he had palsy, and he balled them into fists to keep from shaking. He could feel Pound glancing at him. Every now and again, his Lordship would shoot a look out of the corner of his eye. Finally, he turned his head slightly to face Charlie. Charlie couldn't look back. It didn't matter how rude it was, how much Amy or anyone else would disapprove, he couldn't meet Henry's eye.

"You've been seen to, Shilling?" Henry asked. "You've been patched up? Anything serious?"

Charlie's chin trembled. His eyes were so wet, and his breathing so laboured. It was hard to stay silent when the air wouldn't flow. Impossible to talk. Pound's voice was so soft. So uncharacteristically soft. Charlie wanted to be yelled at. He wanted something to be angry with. Finally, his larynx shaking and his voice thick, he managed a few sticky words.

"I'm not hurt. They stitched me up." His voice sounded strangely high-pitched in his ears, like a scared child lost in the woods.

Henry sighed. It was a deep and powerful sigh. A sound so grave and resonant that Charlie couldn't help but look towards it. Henry was looking at the floor. He stepped sideways and took the chair next to Charlie's, sinking into it like a throne of remorse.

"It's not your fault, Charles," he sighed.

Charlie began to cry. He put his face in his sleeves and erupted into tears, everything he'd held back since arriving. It was his fault. It was absolutely his fault! Having Pound try and relieve him of the responsibility only drove it home.

"It's not your fault, Charlie," Henry insisted, like he could hear what Shilling was thinking. "She's always been like this. Her whole life… girl's so headstrong, if she set her mind to something, there was never a single decision I could talk her out of. Sometimes… I think sometimes I worried it wasn't my place. I let her keep her mother's name, gave her some semblance of autonomy, like… like I was worried she wasn't really my little girl. Like I was scared she'd realise I'm not her real father."

"You are," Shilling muttered, wiping his nose with his sleeve. "You are her father, Pound, and she's always known it."

"But you know what she's like, lad —" Henry sighed.

"I know what she's like," Charlie agreed. "I know she still hasn't told you about France. She's trying to protect you—"

"Shilling," Henry muttered bleakly, "whatever happened between you two over there—"

"Us?" Charlie tipped his head to the side in confusion, wiping his face with a snuffle and staring at Henry. "It's not me, it's her. She hasn't told you because… because we found her birth parents. She met them. All Florin and I did was track down the diamonds, but the thievery was organised by an alias of Liz Florin. We found her with one of her many husbands — Amy's father. Florin... well, you know Florin. She worked it out very quickly."

"She... she said a Marquis..." Henry muttered.

"Jacques Argent," Charlie confirmed. "She found him. He found her. They're staying in touch, and... and she wants to tell you, but she hasn't. She hasn't said anything, Pound, because you're her father. You're the man who raised her. You're the dad she chose, and she doesn't want anything to threaten that."

Henry looked like he was holding himself together with the last threadbare fibre of dignity he possessed, but it was fraying. Charlie recognised the tight lump in his throat and the quiver of his jowls. Henry was staring at the wall again. It was unbelievably fascinating for such a plain wall.

"Then I didn't hear it," Henry breathed in his softest voice yet. "Amy can tell me if... if she..."

"When," Charlie snapped. His voice was weak and hoarse and it took the edge off his retort. "When she wakes up, she can tell you properly."

"Of course," Pound nodded slowly. They sat in silence for a moment. Neither moved or spoke. They barely breathed. Then the softest of sounds came from Henry. A whisper of a chuckle. The tiniest breath of laughter, more the ghost of a memory than the madness of grief, but Charlie glanced at him to be sure. Pound's weary eyes bore unimaginable pain, but a wry smile twisted his lips. "She'd be furious at you if she could see you now," he murmured. His tortured eyes glanced at Charlie. "She gets herself shot, I've got a church still burning in the East End — we'll be lucky if they've got it out by morning, and it's a Goddamn miracle the rookery wasn't close enough to catch — at least two dead bodies, for all I know she's about to be the next one, and we still don't have Kopeck back in custody. God, Amelia would be furious if she could see us sitting around like this."

Charlie watched him, watched the dead eyes and the sharp agony tightening the muscles in his face. Waiting rooms were where souls went to die... but Henry's hadn't come in with him. Henry had walked into this building, into this room, ready to hear that he'd lost his last child. He was still waiting to be told that. If Amy could see them now... he was thinking about her looking down on them, irate at their surrender to helplessness.

And Charlie could still feel her in his arms. He could still feel the weight of her limp body pulling at his shoulders, the wet stiffness of her blood-soaked corset against his hands, the flicker of her racing pulse in her throat. The ghosts of those sensations lingered on his skin, like the scent of her perfume, which had haunted him since the first Jack of Hearts murder.

His relationship with Amelia Florin had always been tied to blood and death. Henry Pound sat beside him like he had always known it would end like this. It was only Charlie who sat in the waiting room... waiting to die. Everyone else had gotten there first. They were waiting on him.

But he wasn't going to die here. Not like this. Not in this room. Not waiting on her. It would be easy to do. If he stayed here, if he waited, if the doctors came out with bad news, it would be easy to stay and die in this room.

But Amy would be furious with him.

Charlie stood up. He pulled his coat from the chair and draped it over his arm. Henry looked up at him, but Charlie stared at the floor. He knew what was about to happen, and he couldn't meet Pound's eye.

"Promise me…" he whispered with newfound steadiness. "Promise me you will be here when she wakes up. I don't want her to be alone."

"I'll be here," Pound swore, ignoring the elephant in the room. "Where are you going, Charles?"

"To clean up this mess," Charlie replied in deadly monotone. "You're right, Pound. She'd be furious. Can't have that. But I can fix it."

Henry was staring at him. A grim spark had come back into his eyes. Charlie knew it was there, but he wouldn't look. If he saw it, they would not be able to pretend anymore. Pound knew that too, and he made his own choice, blinking it away.

"Good," he replied curtly, tapping his cane on the floor and looking to the wall again. "You're right. Can't have you looking like that when she wakes. I'll hold the fort here. You come back once everything's clean and sorted."

"Nothing a relaxing bath, clean shave, and some new clothes can't fix," Charlie muttered.

"I'm sure," Pound agreed in that awfully soft voice.

He, at least, really might not have been certain what

he was agreeing to. Except he was smarter than that. They both knew it. Neither said anything else. Charlie left. He walked the long way around to avoid passing Henry. Neither tried to meet the other's eye. Not now. Not yet.

Not until they'd finished cleaning up.

Dawn was fast approaching and the city was beginning to move. The early birds were looking for worms, or hunkering down. Rain was lashing the city and the bad weather was picking up. John Bullion had seriously considered staying in bed. Any gentleman in their right mind would be tucked up in their blankets. But he wasn't sleeping. Unsettling thoughts had been stirring in his mind ever since the funeral.

He'd known Harry. They'd been friends since they were children. They'd attended law school together. He *knew* Harry. It was madness to think…

And yet the thoughts wouldn't stop.

They just kept piling up at the door to his mind, and no matter how hard he pushed, he couldn't quite keep the door shut. Work felt like the only distraction he had. Even that was deeply flawed. Every now and again, Bullion felt like he caught a glimpse out of the corner of his eye. A spark of Harry's ghost still loitering in the corridors.

He didn't see the body until he'd nearly tripped on it. He had his coat pulled tightly around him with the hood tied shut. The wind was too awful for a hat. Rain whipped at him and he could barely see where he was going in the flickering lamplight. It was only once he made it to the shelter of the stairs outside the Bullion Firm that he could wipe the rain from his face and take in his bearings.

A statue of Justice stood proud on a plinth outside their offices, her blindfolded eyes staring impartially to the horizon. Bullion's lip curled as he saw the drunk slumped at her feet. Foul as the weather might be, it was no excuse for such disrespect — and the stench!

"Oi!" he snapped at them, blinking in the half light and moving to kick them off the steps. His foot connected with a thud and for a second he worried he'd kicked the stair. His toes hurt and the body didn't even move. Not so much as a grunt —

And that was when he saw the blood. It was everywhere. His shoes were covered in it. Not just rain. Blood. Everywhere. All over the stairs. The head… the head was a few stairs away. Bullion had passed it in the rain without realising. He staggered back, gagging. His eyes looked up to Justice, standing resolute with the scales in one hand… and blood dripping from the sword in her other.

Everything hurt and the sounds of a storm raged outside. The scent of work hung in the air. Hospital smells. Linen soap and disinfectant. The gentle clatter of sounds on the ward was drowned out by the raging wind and sprays of rain across the window. Amy woke with a soft groan. She hadn't fallen asleep on shift since her study days. There had been a few times interning when she had done back-to-back shifts and a ten minute break in the supply closet had turned into a twenty minute nap. Not good.

She mumbled and stirred, trying to roll over and completely failing to move. Her whole body ached and she felt dizzy. God, she felt like she'd been drugged. With more difficulty than she expected, she slowly opened her eyes to the half-dark room. It wasn't a supply closet. It was a proper recovery room. The faintest tinge of grey marked dawn through the storm outside.

She blinked hazily, trying to bring her surroundings into focus. She wasn't alone. There was a chair pulled up by the bed and somebody with their arms resting beside her legs and their head resting on their arms. They were snoring gently. She recognised them instantly. Recognised that scruffy straw hair and crooked face.

"Charlie..." she whispered affectionately, reaching out and ruffling his damp hair with a weak hand. She remembered now. She remembered the church and Kopeck and the explosion... and the bullet. She remembered the hideous fear when she had seen Kopeck pull the gun on him, and seen Charlie start to raise his hands... and she hadn't even thought about it. It had been pure instinct. She couldn't let that monster shoot him. Not her Charlie.

He started awake at her touch, blinking dazedly at her.

"Amy…" he muttered, snuffling slightly and rubbing his face as he sat up.

She smiled as she watched him try and compose himself. She remembered him dragging her from the burning church, dragging her through the tunnels… after that her memories got very hazy. He hadn't faltered though. She remembered that much. He had traversed the tunnels fearlessly to save her life… and save her he must have. Here she was, stitched and bandaged, propped up in a hospital bed, trying woozily to come off the anaesthetics.

"You stayed…" she smiled dreamily, reaching her hand out to touch his face again. She couldn't get her elbow off the blankets.

"Of course," he agreed. He reached out and clasped her hand in both of his, bringing her arm back down to the bed and resting it there. Her fingers were cold in his, but he kept her hand clasped between his palms. "Of course, Florin. Of course I stayed." He stroked the backs of her fingers cautiously, like he was stimming, but couldn't let her go. "Your father was here too. He just had to take a call with Commissioner Farthing, but he's around." Charlie was breathing heavily, as though processing trauma, and he wouldn't look her in the eye. His face was drawn and his eyes tight. "We're here. You're going to be okay."

Amy nodded. She was still high on God only knew what they'd given her. That might take some time to wear off. She was dazed and sleepy and there must be important things she wasn't thinking of, but she only had eyes for him. God, he looked so tired. So tired and so worried.

"I am…" she murmured sleepily, wanting to ease his concern. "I am okay, Charlie. I feel fine."

"You'll be all right," he agreed. His voice was soft but there was a hard underlaid edge to it, as though he was daring the world to challenge him. As though he had already done so much, already faced down the tunnels, already done everything and would do more if he had to. Amy smiled dreamily at him.

"Charlie…" she whispered, barely able to keep her eyes open. "Will… will you still be here when I wake up?"

"Of course," he promised, lifting her hand to his face and kissing the backs of her fingers. "I'm not going anywhere, Florin. I'll be here."

"Good," she nodded, her eyes already drooping shut.

She felt him let her hand go and panicked for a moment, but a second later she felt the weight of his arms at her side and the soft warmth of his head as he rested by her again. She reached out, determination compensating for strength, and tangled her fingers in his hair. It was the last thing she felt before sleep took her again.

13

The events of the night before became distant and surreal in the harsh light of day, once the storm had blown over. It was easy to believe it had all been a nightmare. Some hideous, cursed nightmare. Even Florin was in lighter spirits, despite the drugs beginning to wear off. Shilling could have done with some of his own. Anything to alleviate reality. Still, his injuries were minor. His fear for Florin, which had been all-consuming, had eased significantly. Doctors had come and gone and Florin had discussed her condition with them. She should recover admirably, in the fullness of time.

Charlie lounged around her hospital room. He had promised he would stay, and neither of them had discussed how long that promise held for. Either the time would come where it felt right to leave, or he would be made to. For now, he was content waiting.

Then Pound came back. He appeared in the doorway like a wraith or a vulture, clad in black, pale with trauma, but he smiled at his daughter — the kind of smile Shilling hadn't seen on him since Harry's arrest. Charlie still couldn't meet his eye. He did wonder if he would be able to meet Henry Pound's eye ever again.

That was a problem for future Charlie. Still, it was hard to watch Henry and Amy embrace. She was still dopey and lethargic, and the doctors were not prepared to let her out until the end of the day at the earliest. Pound set his hat, coat, and cane across the chair on the other side of the bed and leant over to hold his daughter. Charlie did watch for a moment. He watched and he dwelt.

He dwelt on old pains and new. He missed his own father. He grieved what he had done to Amy and her family. The pain he had caused them was incalculable, although he tried. He stood with his head cocked to the side, twisting his father's ring, trying to calculate his wrongs. But there were too many variables to measure. The scales were too vague. The legal wrongs were easy enough to determine, but the moral wrongs…

How did one measure moral wrongs? And if the answer was guilt, what did that make him?

What did that make Kopeck?

Charlie listened to Florin's endless assurances to her father that she felt fine. Obviously some pain around the injury, but that was to be expected and it certainly wasn't on a scale that warranted concern. Charlie wondered what she'd be saying in a day or two if she didn't keep up the painkillers. He was grateful for the bed and her place in it, like a protective wall between him and Pound.

The only thing Shilling and Pound had discussed when Charlie had returned was his appropriate cleanliness, and the miracle of rain that would have helped to douse the church fire. Nothing else had come up. It should have been comfortable. Charlie felt like the entire world hung between them now. Pound hadn't said anything to him since his Lordship had spoken to the Commissioner.

Outside the room, the hospital was in its usual state of controlled frenzy. Charlie could hear footsteps approaching. Slow, intermittent. He realised someone was looking for the room. Exhaustion and trauma had left him numb and indecisive. There were people outside the door before he'd worked out if he should say something. The knock came before he'd opened his mouth.

"Come in!" Amy called.

Charlie had half expected her friends. He hadn't been paying attention. It was probably understandable, given everything, but he really ought to be better than this. Constables Wilson and Bond appeared in the doorway. Their eyes met and Charlie froze. He thought about running. It would be so easy. He had seven plans in place for if he ever had to flee the country, and all of them were achievable. But the officers' eyes glazed over him and turned to the two at the bed.

"Your Lordship?" Bond inquired. "You said you wanted to see the file as soon as it was available."

"Thank you, Constable," Pound straightened up and approached them. "That was... surprisingly expedient."

"Highest priority, all things considered," Wilson replied, handing over a brown folder.

Charlie cocked his head to the side and scanned the text on the front. It was exactly what he thought it was.

"What's going on?" Amy asked, struggling to sit

properly in the bed.

Charlie moved to her without thinking, helping to prop her up on the pillows before he even realised where his hands were, and that there were witnesses. No one else seemed to notice. That was odd. Usually, social absurdities were the only thing he was the last to notice. As he moved away from her, Florin took his hand. He hadn't the heart to pull it from her grasp, and once again, no one seemed to notice.

"Kopeck's case file," Charlie muttered to her. Someone had to answer, and it wasn't like he was unaware.

"Have you found her yet?" Amy grimaced at the police.

"Yep," Wilson nodded.

"Both pieces," Bond added.

"Both pieces...?" Amy echoed. Her eyes widened and she let go of Shilling's hand. He stepped back from her gratefully, eager to be away from any stray threads of attention. "If you found anything that passes for her burnt body in the church, don't believe it!"

"No, Doctor..." Bond shook her head grimly. "It's Kopeck, and it wasn't anywhere near the church."

"Found her in Westminster, outside one of them old law firms," Wilson added. "Decapitated by God."

"De-what-ed by what?!" Amy exclaimed.

Despite everything, Charlie couldn't help but feel his own eyebrows hit his hairline. Even for those two buffoons, that was a new level of preposterous. It wasn't nearly as farcical as what came next.

"Decapitated by God," Lord Pound repeated with

undue consideration, leafing through the file. "My, you two have certainly put together a compelling argument for something so outlandish. When I spoke to Farthing this was not quite what I… but, well, I suppose… Well. It's something. God help us once this leaks to the media. I know the early morning papers missed the story, but the body was found by a citizen, and I imagine the evening papers will talk of nothing else."

"Decapitated by WHAT?!" Amy repeated, trying to pull herself from the bed.

Charlie quickly dashed back and tried to ease her back onto the pillows.

"God," Bond replied with a completely straight face. "Or maybe Lady Justice — but that would definitely be seen as an act of God."

"Makes sense to me," Wilson shrugged. "Kopeck escaped death row, killed a little girl and a vicar, blew up a church, and shot the daughter of the Lord Chief Justice. God saw it, went 'that's enough of that' and thwack — off with her head."

Amy turned, very slowly and painstakingly, to face Charlie. Her green eyes did not have enough morphine to cloud them and seemed to be demanding someone explain the reality she had awoken in. Given the absurdity of the report they were listening to, Charlie found the will to simply shrug. If this was madness, he would join her.

"Daddy," Amy turned back to Pound, "you cannot be serious."

"Unprecedented though it may be in our time, the evidence supports it," Pound shrugged.

Charlie snorted. He couldn't help himself. Pound was concerningly good at playing stupid. So were the constables, although there was every chance they weren't playing. He couldn't help but wonder what they were doing with a case like this anyway.

"You can have a look if you want," Bond offered, motioning the file Pound held towards Amy. "You were consulting on the case to catch her anyway. Looks like divine intervention had a say in the outcome. Glad you're all right, by the way."

Amy held out her hand for the file. Pound glanced at her. His shrewd eyes took in her glare and his lips pursed in a small frown.

"Amelia, darling, you ought to be resting," he chided. "You don't need to concern yourself with all this—"

"Give it," she ordered. "Don't be condescending, Daddy. Show me."

Pound maintained his frown, but he seemingly couldn't maintain his stance. Charlie realised he was going to cave a second before it happened, and slowly slunk back from the bed. He glimpsed the file as Pound handed it over. The tiniest flash of text and images. He turned away and moved to the window, looking at the sunshine drying the rain from the leaves outside. He knew what that file said. He knew what was in there.

Kopeck had been found beheaded at the foot of the statue of Justice. Her blood was on the sword. An obvious staging by someone with a taste for theatrics, as even the constables were quick to point out. Except...

Except no one knew what weapon had caused the

wound, if not the sword. It was a clean cut. One slice, straight through. Kopeck was a huge woman, tall and strong. There would be few people, if any, who could have taken her head clean off if she were standing. Even if someone had been standing on the statue above her, the nature of the statue and the placement of the body meant there was no space for anyone to get a good swing. No one could cut through a neck like that without a decent swing of force behind them. If she wasn't standing, who got her on the ground? Why were there no marks made by a weapon slicing through her into the floor or plinth?

Then there was the blood spray to consider. It was uninhibited. There was no evidence to suggest someone had been blocking the spray. It started at the statue, as though Kopeck had backed into Justice herself and the Lady of Righteousness had drawn her sword, set it to Kopeck's throat, and seen the terms of her sentence served. There wasn't a single piece of evidence to suggest anyone else had been there.

And motive? Motive made half of London potential suspects, but who had the time, ability, and opportunity to kill a woman like Kopeck?

Who had even managed to find her?

Charlie stood at the window for a long time. He could feel the air in the room chill. At no point did he turn. He didn't want to see. He couldn't look. Meeting Pound's eye was no longer a concern. The real question, the gut-wrenching issue before him now, was how could he ever meet her eye? How could he ever look at Amy again and expect her not to recoil. He stood at the window and waited for her to state the obvious.

Eventually, she gave a small sigh, and he heard the folder close. He pressed his eyes shut and leant on the window frame.

"It's a miracle," she admitted softly. "I wouldn't have believed it if I hadn't seen it. Like something from the Book of Magdalane. God's own justice. Maybe she got tired of waiting."

"Doesn't fill you with confidence for the system though, does it?" Wilson sniffed, taking the file back and sharing a frown with Bond. "Makes you worry a little bit… if we're doing such a piss poor job that God herself has to step up and do some divine smiting."

"Bloody good argument for capital punishment, though," Bond grimaced.

Charlie winced.

"Thank you for your time, Constables," Pound dismissed their speculation. "You will keep me informed of any new developments?"

"Of course, Your Lordship," Bond bowed them from the room. The constables were nearly at the door when they backed into someone new coming to knock.

"Lord Pound?" the newcomer peeked in. "Sorry to disturb you, there's another call from the Commissioner—"

"God give me strength," Pound muttered. "Amy, darling, give me a minute. I'll be right back."

It seemed altogether too quickly they were alone in the room again. Pound even shut the door behind him. Charlie still didn't turn. Not until she bid him, and then he couldn't refuse.

"Charlie…?" Amy addressed him, her voice so plaintive it was almost a whisper.

He left the window and returned to the bedside. Amy held her hand up to him and he took it in his again. He had half a mind to kiss her fingers again, but it wouldn't be appropriate. That much he could still deduce. He ran his thumb across her nails and kept his eyes there. She was looking at him. He could feel it, but he couldn't meet her eye.

"Sit with me, Charlie," she requested.

He pulled the chair closer and sank down into it, still holding her hand. Finally, she was the one who broke the silence.

"You didn't look at the file," she commented. "I would have thought you'd be interested in such a case."

"Kopeck's gone," he replied. "It's over. That's enough."

"Not tempting fate, huh?"

"Something like that," he agreed. His thumb traced backwards and forwards over her fingers and he watched the movement, hoping it was as soothing to her as it was to him.

"Charlie…" She said his name again and he could hear the hesitation and uncertainty in her voice. She wasn't sure she wanted to say this, and he knew what was coming. "You… you know, Charlie… when… when I first looked at the file… Kopeck… You know, my first thoughts were that, given her injuries, and possibly with the help of opiates, such an execution could have been carried out with something like pottery wire, if the killer caught her from behind the statue."

They both sat in absolute silence. Charlie wasn't breathing. He knew she'd covered for him. Just like she'd taken a bullet for him. He pressed his lips together to keep them from trembling, and tried very hard not to think about the way he was killing her slowly. First with Harry, then France, now Kopeck… little wounds piling up. Once he had his body under control, he very gradually and silently let out the breath he'd been holding and spoke in a calm and even tone.

"Well," he licked his lips delicately, "once you're better, you can take your findings to Wilson and Bond. I'm sure they'd appreciate the insight."

"I don't think so," Florin smiled softly, shaking her head. "Honestly, people are known to say the silliest things coming off anaesthetics. I'm sure I'm no different. Besides, after everything that happened, I'd say I'm much too close to the case to help with it, and Wilson and Bond are doing just fine."

Charlie had no idea what to say to that. Despite her claims regarding the anaesthetics, she knew exactly what she was doing. Exactly what she was saying. It would have been wrong to fight her. But he didn't know what else to do either. The weight of the choice before him was looming, growing… soon it would be too huge to ignore. He was going to have to face it.

"Charlie…" Amy whispered.

He looked up. He met her eyes. They had to be the most beautiful eyes in the world. Faerie green eyes in her brown face surrounded by black freckles. They were so full of wisdom and understanding. So full of sympathy. Looking at them now made him want to cry.

Looking at her now made him understand what he had to do… but after everything else he'd done, he wasn't sure he was strong enough to do it.

"Go home, Charlie," she told him. "Have Rebecca make you a pot of tea. Get some sleep. You look dead on your feet."

He nodded meekly. That was sage advice. But he couldn't go. He couldn't leave… not knowing what had to happen next.

"I'll be fine," she promised.

The words hit him like a wave, but not a forceful one. They didn't bowl him over. It wasn't a storm. More a gentle tide, teasing around his ankles and then gently pulling the sand out from beneath his feet. Eroding the ground that held him up.

"Yes, you will," he agreed, standing slowly and letting go of her hand.

"Charlie!" She must have seen the look in his eye. She'd always been good at that. Much better than he was. She had that knack for reading people.

He leant over the bed, cupping her cheek with his hand and gently kissing her forehead. He knew it was dismissive, more so than he'd ever wanted to be, but he hoped it was affectionate too.

"Don't you dare," she hissed, grabbing him by the lapels of his coat.

He couldn't stop her as she pulled his lips to hers, gluing him to her kiss. He didn't even try. His hand still rested against her face. It was hard not to kiss her back. He wasn't sure he managed it. When he pulled away, he did so with a whisper.

"Goodbye, Florin."

She didn't say anything. She didn't yell or throw anything. He didn't even know if she wanted to, although he was certain he could feel her anger radiating beneath the waves of his own regret. He didn't look back as he left the room, shutting the door soundlessly behind him.

He stalked carefully down the passage, making himself invisible in the crowds, vigilantly taking the paths he knew wouldn't pass Henry. Florin was right. He needed a rest and some tea, and certainly to check in on his sisters and his friends at the bakery. He needed to get his life back. He needed to do all those things and he needed to keep Florin safe. He needed to stop endangering her and ruining her life. The best way to do that was to stay well away from her.

Thus concludes *A Dalliance with Grief* Book Three of the *Shilling & Florin Mysteries*. The story continues in
BOOK FOUR:
THE CASE OF SILVER & SOVEREIGN

Did you enjoy this book?

Please consider leaving a review for it on Amazon or Goodreads. Every positive review allows me to spend more time writing books for you to enjoy!

katehaleyauthor/amazon

OTHER BOOKS BY KATE HALEY

Welcome to the Inbetween

The Light After Earth

Like the Heroes of Old

Shilling & Florin Mysteries

1. The Jack of Hearts Murders

2. The Thief & the Marquis

3. A Dalliance with Grief

4. The Case of Silver & Sovereign

5. A Cold & Bitter Revenge

6. The Pen & the Blade

7. Blood & Bells

8. Tarnished Silver

The War of the North Saga

Footsteps into the Unfamiliar (short story collection)

1. Steel & Stone

2. Magic in the Marshes

3. Forest of Ghosts

4. Women of the Woods

5. Spirit & Sand

6. The Prince and the Witch

7. Gods & Dragons

The Vincent Temple Trilogy (+ Prequel)

Path of Dreaming Souls (Prequel)

1. Gateway to Dark Stars

2. Tomb of Endless Night

3. Fortress of the Shadow Reich

ABOUT THE
AUTHOR

Kate Haley is a speculative fiction author who works predominantly in fantasy and horror.

While currently content to fill their days with writing and table-top RPGs, their grander plans involve world domination. Something akin to the tyranny of the greatest city atop the Disc would be an acceptable standard. They believe a super-villainous overlord would be an upgrade, given that our current villains lack style and imagination.

After all, super-villainy requires Presentation.

If you like their references, consider visiting their website www.katehaleyauthor.com for short fictions and merchandise, and join the mailing list for early access and exclusive cool stuff.

You can also get in touch through the website regarding their work, your position in future slave armies, or a general interest in all things nerdy and wonderful.